Devil Take Me

by

Karilyn Bentley

A Demon Huntress Novel

Devil Take Me

Cover Art by *Diana Carlile*

The Wild Rose Press, Inc.
PO Box 708
Adams Basin, NY 14410-0708
Visit us at www.thewildrosepress.com

Publishing History
First Mainstream Paranormal Edition, 2018
Print ISBN 978-1-5092-1890-5
Digital ISBN 978-1-5092-1891-2

A Demon Huntress Novel
Published in the United States of America

A vision of an auburn-haired man

dressed in dark trousers and a gray button-down, appears in my head. He sits on my closed toilet lid, watching me sleep in the full tub, watching as my head slides closer to the waterline.

It must be a dream. How else can I be asleep and still see the bathroom, my sleeping self and the man? A dream. Only a dream. His voice is nothing more than my imaginings.

And yet I feel the need to answer. To deny his words.

I'm not listening to you. I make an effort to rebuke the voice, refusing to take what it offers, refusing to admit its enticing pull.

Oh, but you are. He leans forward, resting his elbows on his knees, his gaze firmly affixed to my face. *You contemplate my words. You seek the rest only I can give.*

Yeah, right. Not buying it, buster. Although I'm starting to want what he offers. I'll never admit it to Mystery Man. *What can a figment of my imagination really do?*

I am not a figment. He smiles, his lips pulling away from straight, white teeth.

Despite the warm water, a chill runs down my spine. He holds out his hand.

Come. Take my hand. Rest. Leave your problems behind.

Praise for Karilyn Bentley

"[*DEMON LORE* is an] action-packed tale of demons, guardians and magical abilities."

~Linda Green at Fresh Fiction

"Fantastic start to a new series."

~Annetta Sweetko at Fresh Fiction

~*~

"…the story [in *DEMON KISSED*] is a snarky, fast-paced romp that kept me reading straight through the afternoon…"

~Katie O'Sullivan at Read, Write, Repeat

"The world is interesting and is explained well and the story is full of action, suspense and a bit of romantic drama."

~Urban Fantasy Investigations

~*~

"I also love how the author paints a picture in my mind by these spellbinding sentences [in *DEMON CURSED*]."

~Booktalk with Eileen

Dedications

A big thank you goes to Kathy Ivan
for her wonderful plotting help
as well as to Carrie Hamlin and J.C. McKenzie,
beta readers extraordinaire.
Without you, ladies,
this book would never have come about.
~*~
And to my husband for his feedback and support.
I love you more than words can say.

Chapter One

Whoever said tomorrow is another day must never have awakened to the mother of all hangovers. *Unlike me*. Which happens when you drink half a bottle of whiskey and smoke your twin brother's weed to escape your horrible screw-up. I swear sand coats my mouth, swelling my tongue, drying my throat. Light trickles through the blinds, digging painful holes into my brain.

I need water.

But getting it would defeat the purpose of punishment. And punishment is what I deserve. Punishment for killing a human.

I, Gin Champagne Crawford, killed a fellow human being.

Killing demons and minions is one thing. As the world's newest *Justitian*, or demon huntress as I call my new gig, I'm expected to blast those things back to Hell, or wherever it is they go once their bodies disintegrate. Humans, though, humans I'm supposed to leave alive.

Donny isn't alive. Not at all. His body is, well, probably at the morgue by now.

A tear escapes my squeezed shut eyes. *Donny. Mr. Football*. A player known for his charitable contributions and face-time with the media. And the man who slept with my twin's ex-girlfriend. Still, he didn't deserve to die.

Although Donny did align himself with Rahab, the demon of pride. Well, sort of align himself. More like Donny considered becoming a minion. Strongly considered. Which means I might have needed to end his life one of these days, but he wasn't a minion when I accidentally shoved my sword through his heart.

I killed a human who might have been saved.

Another tear squeezes past my closed eyes as the events of yesterday flood my mind.

To start things off, my twin, T, said he never wanted to see me again and stormed out the door. Then Smythe, my mage-guardian and most recent lover, thought I had a thing going on with Donny and pulled a disappearing act.

Okay, maybe Donny did deserve a sword through his heart for forcing a kiss on me right when Smythe walked in Donny's private room at Club Monster in Dallas.

To cap the day, my hidden stash of whiskey, the bottle I kept to prove I could avoid hard liquor and stay on the narrow road of only beer, sits on the nightstand almost empty. Last night, the smooth slide of liquid down my throat pushed back the memory loop of my terrible, horrible, no good, fucked up day faster than my sword cut into Donny.

Until I woke.

Now, my memories threaten my sanity, along with a healthy dose of bruised pride and complete shame, made worse by the raging headache and roiling stomach.

What kind of person kills a human?

The kind who'd down half a bottle of whiskey and a couple of blunts rather than face her mistakes.

I am a horrible person.

Maybe you should end it all. Maybe you should drink the rest of the bottle, ensuring complete oblivion. Drink. Come to me.

The deep voice slithers across my mind, soothing frayed endings, calming my racing heart.

What. The. Fuck?

My eyes pop open, searching for the source of the voice. Bad idea. Another dagger of sunlight attempts a lobotomy, forcing me to slam my lids shut. Why am I in T's room instead of mine? A question which isn't nearly as important as, is someone else in the room with me?

I hold my breath, trying to discern if someone broke in, but the only noise I hear is the throb of my heartbeat pounding in my ears.

Right. As if a burglar would break into my house and watch me sleep. A demon, though…

My eyes try for another round of open and squeeze shut. Then open and squint. No one in front of me, standing next to the bed as I lie on my side. Maybe behind me? I roll. Huge mistake. My stomach contents threaten a reappearance. Clapping a hand over my mouth, I roll back the other way, fall off the bed and heave onto the floor.

At least the floor isn't carpeted, which makes for easier cleanup.

Like some effed-up perk, the fall shakes loose the memory otherwise known as the cherry on top of my fucked-up day. Zagan, my demon "friend" telling me I'm a loser. I look at the puddle of puke and decide the demon had a point.

Only a loser pukes all over her brother's bedroom

floor. Speaking of brothers, why am I in T's room?

A memory spins into my mind, a memory of me cradling my whiskey bottle while sitting on T's bed, smoking his joints. Yeah, definitely a loser.

Drink. Come to me.

The deep voice again echoes inside my head. Not in the room. Inside me.

A hallucination? After last night's pot-and-booze-a-polooza I wouldn't be surprised.

Both T and Smythe can talk to me telepathically. Should someone else be added to that short list?

Which option is scarier? Whichever one, I'm pretty sure it's the winner.

I rest my head against the cool wood floor, immediately wishing I hadn't. Yuck. Smelly. I need to clean up.

Using the bed as leverage, I shove upright. The room spins, then stabilizes. I push to my feet, clap a hand over my mouth and high-tail it to the hall bathroom. After flushing, washing my hands, throwing water on my face, and sipping the cool, over-chlorinated liquid straight from the faucet, I stare in the mirror.

But only for a second. Enough to see streaked makeup, sleep lines on my cheek, a bad case of bed-hair and bloodshot eyes. Double yuck.

Or maybe quadruple? Math never was my thing.

I stumble out of the bathroom, down the hall to my bedroom, strip off my clothes and climb into my shower. Upright proves an unsteady adventure, so I turn off the shower and stop up the tub. Once the water fills the tub, I sit down and lean my head against the rim, letting my eyes slide shut.

How do I move past what I've done? I've messed up in so many ways, all in one day. Is there a reset option to start yesterday over?

Of course not. Yesterday is done. Finished. The past is written in stone.

How do I scratch away the writing? How do I move forward?

Come to me. This time when the voice speaks, I keep my eyes closed, sinking into the deep timbre as if it were my own personal floatation device. *All your problems will disappear. Just relax. Let the water bring you to me.*

Maybe I should do as the mysterious voice says. Let go. Slip away. Never worry again.

Wait a minute. Since when do I listen to mysterious voices? Hell, I didn't even listen to my own internal voice last night telling me drinking half a bottle of whiskey might be a bad idea, why would I listen to some hallucination?

Not a hallucination.

A vision of an auburn-haired man dressed in dark trousers and a gray button-down, appears in my head. He sits on my closed toilet lid, watching me sleep in the full tub, watching as my head slides closer to the waterline.

It must be a dream. How else can I be asleep and still see the bathroom, my sleeping self and the man? A dream. Only a dream. His voice is nothing more than my imaginings.

And yet I feel the need to answer. To deny his words.

I'm not listening to you. I make an effort to rebuke the voice, refusing to take what it offers, refusing to admit its enticing pull.

Oh, but you are. He leans forward, resting his elbows on his knees, his gaze firmly affixed to my face. *You contemplate my words. You seek the rest only I can give.*

Yeah, right. Not buying it, buster. Although I'm starting to want what he offers. I'll never admit it to Mystery Man. *What can a figment of my imagination really do?*

I am not a figment. He smiles, his lips pulling away from straight, white teeth.

Despite the warm water, a chill runs down my spine. He holds out his hand.

Come. Take my hand. Rest. Leave your problems behind.

His fingers beckon, a gentle call to relax. I shouldn't take him up on his offer, but maybe he's right. Maybe resting is all I need. Maybe I should listen to a mysterious man sitting on my toilet lid, begging me to take his hand.

Maybe he really can take me away from myself, from my pain, from the knowledge I majorly screwed up.

I open my eyes, meeting the man's gaze. Yep, the man sits on my toilet lid, but I'm still not convinced this is anything more than a dream. And in my dreams, I can have all the relaxation and relief from my screwed-up life I can get. I reach out a hand to him. His smile widens into a sinister grin.

Right before he grips my palm, the bathroom door slams open, ricocheting against the wall. The man disappears as if he never existed, leaving my hand hanging mid-air. My twin, T, stands in the doorway, his icy glare chilling the room.

I let loose with a little squeak and yank the shower curtain closed while the anger in T's low voice reverberates against the walls.

"What the fuck are you doing, Gin?"

"Taking a bath?" I poke my head outside the curtain.

"Like hell." His fingers whiten as he grips the doorknob. "Who was talking to you?"

"You came back." Maybe things aren't so bad. My twin returned.

Of course he still looks as mad as when he left.

Things apparently remain bad between us.

His jaw flexes. "Who were you talking to?"

"No one was here. Just a dream."

"Again. Like hell. You think I couldn't hear him too, calling to you? His voice came right through our mental link. Was he the fucking grim reaper, or what?"

I focus on my twin's words, which is a little hard to do with a stupid hangover.

Could T be right? Was the grim reaper chatting me up while sitting on my toilet? What were the chances?

Slim or none?

"Gin?" T's voice slides lower, calm and steady, a virtual growl. Not a good sign. His next words confirm it. "Why does the house reek of weed and booze?"

Damn. Busted. I swallow in a vain attempt to clear away the sand-like substance coating my throat. It doesn't work. I hang my head, my voice little more than a whisper.

"Don't go in your room. I need to clean it."

"Shit. What the hell, Gin? What the hell?"

My twin, short on words, but what he does say,

sums up things nicely.

T slaps a palm against the door jamb, making me jump. "Get out of the bath, get dressed, and get your punk ass to the kitchen."

With those words, he slams the door shut behind him.

A tear slides down my cheek. I scrub it away. Why did I think grabbing a dream man's hand would make all my problems disappear?

And why did T think my dream was of the grim reaper? Would a grim reaper appear as a dream man instead of a spirit? Wasn't the creature nothing more than a fantasy made up to explain how people died? I didn't die. I'm pretty damn messed up, but nowhere close to dead.

So why did my twin get so upset over a dream?

Chapter Two

By the time I stumble into the kitchen, T has started the coffee brewing. Usually I love coffee, drinking several extra-large mugs of the liquid gold, stopping only when the pot runs dry. Today, instead of its normal welcoming smell, the odor turns my stomach. This time, nothing makes a repeat appearance.

Thank goodness.

My brother stands with his hands resting against the counter in front of the sink, staring out the window as if the neighborhood street holds all the answers. Tension tightens his muscles, radiates into the kitchen in a warm rush of energy. T upset is never a good thing.

Why was he back? Perhaps he realized he was wrong to blame me for his ex-girlfriend Jackie's death?

After all, it wasn't my fault a crazy serial killer minion stalked her. Nonetheless, his actions yesterday hurt all the same. My twin and I are—or should I say, were—close.

"Hey."

At the sound of my voice, he turns, eyes narrowed, jaw tense. "Are you punishing me for leaving yesterday?"

"No, not you." I pause, stare at my feet for a second before meeting his eyes. "What you said hurt," a hell of a lot worse than I'd ever say, "but me getting trashed is not your fault."

Never his fault. Only mine. Playing the blame game gets me nowhere.

Something I should have realized earlier in my screwed-up life.

His gaze drops to the ground before meeting mine. "I shouldn't have stormed off."

Damn straight. An opinion I keep to myself. Instead, I shrug and squint, wishing for a pair of sunglasses. I never realized how bright this kitchen really was until a team of painful, light-induced jackhammers took up residence in my skull.

"It's okay. I don't like us to be mad at each other."

He steps forward, wraps me in his arms. As soon as he enfolds me in a hug, a sense of calm flows through me, through us. A perk of being twins, our touch gives each other a peaceful relaxed feeling. One of the few times in my life I feel this way is when T gives me a hug.

Or Smythe wraps me in his arms.

Nope, not gonna think about Smythe and how we could have been a couple. My damn mentor wouldn't listen to reason. I don't want him back.

Despite T's arms around me, what feels like little shards of glass shatter my heart, giving evidence of my lie.

T steps back, eyes narrowed. "What happened? If it wasn't me, what caused you to slip?"

I sigh, step around him, heading toward the bottle of ibuprofen in the cabinet. Do I want to tell him what a loser I am?

As if he doesn't already know. The house smells like pot, spilled booze and puke, a clear giveaway.

I pull out a glass, fill it with water and down the

round, brown pills.

"My life fell in the shitter after you left."

He gestures to the steaming pot of coffee. "Pour yourself some and tell me about it."

Even though the smell makes my stomach roll, I do as he says, working on the assumption what worked in the past for hangovers will work in the present. Filling my extra-large mug, I head to the living room couch where thankfully the blinds remain closed. The couch's springs squeak as I sit.

T sits on the other end, turned toward me, leg bent at the knee.

I take a wary sip and a swallow. My stomach settles a bit. Actually, more than a bit. As if it's been an entire day after a binge as opposed to hours. No doubt a perk of wearing the *justitia*, a fancy name for the bracelet attached to my wrist.

Justitias give their wearers super-healing powers. Which doesn't mean we can't be hurt or even killed. While healing us faster than we'd normally heal on our own, life-threatening injuries still require outside help. The Agency, the organization in charge of the *Justitians* and their guardian mages, employs dozens of healers for demon and minion induced injuries.

But not even the healers can save every injured *Justitian* who walks through the doors.

T clears his throat.

Right. Stop wandering down rabbit holes of avoidance, Gin.

"After you left yesterday, Smythe was called to the Agency. He told me to wait for him before we confronted Donny."

"Why would you talk with Donny? So he fucked

11

Jackie—" At my wide-eyed expression, he interrupts himself. "What, you thought I didn't know? Why do you think we broke up?"

I ignore his question, opting to get to the heart of the matter. "I killed Donny."

His eyes round, mouth agape. Yeah, it might not have been the best way to tell him, but the confession popped out before I could stop it.

"Say what?"

I swallow while staring at my white fingers clutching my mug. "I killed Donny Merryweather."

My voice hitches on the last syllable of his name. I swallow again.

"Damn. Over Jackie?"

My gaze meets his. "Don't be ridiculous. I was aiming for a demon and he got in the way."

"Where was Smythe?"

"He got mad at me and stormed out."

T stiffens. *Son of a bitch* slams into my mind, courtesy of our telepathic link. He swallows as if the motion will wipe away his projected thought. When he speaks, his voice shows none of his anger. "Why don't you start at the beginning?"

Once again my gaze drops to my coffee mug, to the steam spiraling out the top. Reliving my horrid day out loud makes me feel like an even bigger loser.

Although, don't they say talk therapy helps purge one's conscious?

Purging hurts.

"You left. Then Smythe got called to the Agency. He said for me to stay put, but I knew I could get the info out of Donny."

"What info?"

"Sorry. We thought Donny had something to do with the serial killer. The one who targeted Jackie. Are you sure you're okay? You two were together for, like, a year. I thought you cared about her."

T's jaw tenses as his gaze skitters everywhere but on me. "I'm cool."

"T…" I don't need to hop into his head to know "cool" is not his current state of mind.

"Okay, fine. It hurts. Bad. I was pissed off she left, even though I knew the relationship was over. But I didn't want her hurt. God. She's dead. Dead, Gin. That hurts." He pauses. Runs a hand over his head. "I guess this is how you felt after Blake died."

Blake. My on-again-off-again friend with benefits. Until Smythe came along, Blake was the one guy who understood me. Or should I say, sort of understood me. At any rate, we became good friends despite my empathic touch-and-see problem/ability, which didn't faze him in the slightest. He even learned to project a beach scene when I kissed him. Which was wonderful not to have a glimpse into another's mind while enjoying an intimate moment. The demon Jezebeth killed him as revenge for me killing her regiment of minions shortly after I became a demon huntress.

Damn demons.

"Yeah. It hurts to lose someone you care about." Real deep thought there, Gin. Geez. But it's the only comforting thing my hungover mind spits out.

"Yeah." He massages the bridge of his nose, a quick gesture meant to soothe his mind. Or buy time while he thinks of what to say next. "Back to Donny. You really took him out? Damn it, the Armadillos are gonna suck this year."

I shoot him a brief glare, but otherwise ignore his prediction about our local NFL team's chances at the Super Bowl. While watching the steam circle my mug, I continue my tale.

"As I was saying, I thought I could find out what Donny knew about the serial killer. Smythe," my voice hitches and I swallow, "Smythe thought Donny was the killer."

"Donny might be a man-ho but he's not a killer." T shakes his head.

"Yeah, that's what I said. And I knew I could get him to talk. All the dead women were with him before dying. Anyway, when I got to the club, Donny had his guard bring me back to his private suite. When I got there, he was all flowers and proposals and trying to get me into bed. Like I'm going to nail him at the club. Or anywhere for that matter. And Smythe and I are," another hitch causes me to clear my throat, "were together. And I don't—didn't—think of Donny that way. I went to shove his flowers back in his face, when he grabbed me and planted one right on my lips." I take a deep breath as I tell T what happened next. "Smythe walked in and saw us."

"Oh. It didn't go so well, eh?"

"That's the understatement of the month. The jackass wouldn't even listen to me. He assumed I wanted Donny over him, told me I was an adult and could do what I wanted and stormed off. Naturally I started to go after him and explain, but then Rahab, the leader of the pride demons, strolled in with his minion, who happened to be the actual serial killer, so I had other things to do besides chase down Smythe."

T's eyes widen. "Did you nail the bastard who

killed Jackie?"

"Yep." I draw a line across my throat, indicating my *justitia's* sword chopped the minion's head right off. "Unfortunately, the demon started to turn Donny into a minion, but when I went to stab Rahab, I missed, and killed Donny instead." A memory returns: Rahab offering me to Donny in exchange for him becoming a minion, which led to Donny accepting the minion status. Maybe the prick did deserve to die. Nah, I take it back. He deserved to be bitch-slapped, but not killed.

"Oh, man, I'm sorry." T pauses, brow wrinkling and relaxing. "I don't understand why Donny would want to be a minion. He's already famous."

My jaw tenses. "Donny wanted me. And since I wouldn't have him, he made a deal with the demon to become a minion in exchange for me. Rahab must feed off pride. You can't tell me Donny wasn't full of himself."

T nods. "Okay, then. Donny was more of a bastard than I thought. You offed the minion. Missed stabbing the demon. Then what?"

"The demon got the upper hand and knocked me out."

T's eyes widen then narrow. I rush to continue before he can voice his usual I-don't-like-you-getting-hurt comment.

"I'm fine."

He raises a brow.

"Really. I was fine. But Smythe wouldn't answer his phone, so I had to call the Agency's emergency cleanup crew who made the scene look like someone else killed Donny."

"You saying you aren't going to be a suspect in his

death?"

"Yep. They blamed everything on the guy who helped the serial killer minion hunt and kill the victims. You know, the dude who tried to kidnap me? Well, he got what was coming to him. And it got a potential killer off the street."

"And Smythe? Did he ever call you back?"

I shake my head. "Never." I swipe a tear off my cheek.

T grunts. "Told you he'd hurt you. He's not good enough for you."

I sniff. "In your opinion, is anyone?"

T blinks, once, twice. A crooked grin turns one corner of his lips. "Damn straight. No one's good enough for my sis."

"Uh-huh." I return his grin. "Keep that up and I'll be living a lonely life."

He chuckles before turning serious. "I see why you had a bad day."

"And it didn't end at the club. Zagan, my *justitia's* friend," and in a weird way, my friend too, although I don't want to admit it to T, "said I was a loser since I failed to kill Rahab."

"Yeah." He rolls his eyes. "That would definitely push you over the ledge. Having a demon call you a loser."

"I killed a human, T. I killed Donny."

"And Smythe acted like an ass."

"Yeah. I thought we had something. Something…" my voice trails into nothing as tears escape my eyes. I hate crying. But I can't stop.

The look of betrayal turning Smythe's face into hard stone. My sword thrusting into Donny's chest. The shocked look on the football star's face as he dropped dead on the floor.

I'm stronger than this.

But the tears refuse to go away. My breath comes in little hitching sobs as T wraps his arms around me. This time, not even his embrace brings peace.

****

Hours later, after calling in sick for my shift at Blue Forest ER, being written up for calling in late—my first write-up damn it—and cleaning the mess in T's room, I sit on the couch alone, watching the news coverage of Donald Merryweather, aka Donny Football's, untimely death at Club Monster. I should turn it off. But I leave it running on the off-chance repeat exposure dulls the pain.

The expression on Donny's face as my sword slams into his chest replays in my mind. Shock. Horror. Fear.

In my effort to save him from becoming a minion, I ended his life.

Can I ever forgive myself?

At least T and I are solid again. And he's making me dinner, although I'm not sure I can choke down food. The *justitia* healed me, so I am no longer hungover, but the entity living along my nerves can't touch the emotional turmoil in my head or the sickening ache in my chest.

Some demon huntress I am.

The news changes from coverage about Donny to some Dallas deacon who offed himself, surprising his friends and family. What a joyful broadcast.

"Hey, turn that shit off and come keep me company," T yells from the kitchen.

After a pause, I do as he says, hitting the off button on the remote while getting to my feet with all the speed of a cold slug. If only Smythe were here. Maybe he could make me feel better about Donny. Provided there was a way to feel better.

But noooo. Smythe refused to listen when I tried to explain why he caught Donny giving me an unwanted kiss. Which meant my mentor wasn't there when I fought Rahab. When I killed Donny. Instead, Smythe was off having a pity party.

Quicker than I could take a step toward T and the kitchen, my anger ignites, morphing from sorrow into rage.

How dare Aidan Smythe leave me alone to face a demon. His job as a guardian mage is to protect his assigned *Justitian*—me. Not abandon me to fight a demon alone because of some misplaced sense of betrayal.

Bastard.

I stomp into the kitchen. Rage I can deal with. Rage washes away my sense of loss, my despair. At least for the moment.

Looks like I have a to-do item not involving self-doubt and pity. Call Smythe and give him a piece of my mind.

"You seem better. Less sad."

"Just realized Smythe is being a self-centered bastard."

T opens his mouth, immediately snapping it shut, as if afraid to voice his thoughts. "Mmmm."

"He left me to deal with things on his own. He refused to let me explain what he saw. He thought the worst of me." I bang a hand on the counter. The sting only serves to ratchet up my anger.

As if it can get any worse.

"He was hurt."

I raise a brow at my twin's serious expression. "Wait. Are you actually siding with him?"

"Of course not. Just pointing out the obvious."

"Doesn't excuse him from acting like a jerk."

"True." T turns to the stove, stirring what looks like a pot of bagged vegetables fresh out of the freezer. "But maybe he was hurt. Sounds like something I'd do."

"Be an ass? Leave me to defend myself? I think not."

"I meant it's something I'd do if I saw my girlfriend kissing another guy."

"I'm not his girlfriend." Which isn't to say I wouldn't mind the position. Before he left me alone in a fight against a demon, that is. Now I'm not so sure.

"You're his something."

I cross my arms and lean against the doorjamb. "Not anymore. Thanks for the reminder."

T looks at me, a contrite expression crossing his face. "Sorry. Didn't mean to upset you. Just pointing out the obvious."

"So you've said. And it's fine. I never stopped being upset at him. You know what? I'm going to call him again. Maybe he's cooled off."

"Mmmm."

T turns back to the stove as I march into my bedroom. After finding my phone in my purse, I unlock the screen, hoping for a message from my absentee mentor.

No such luck.

Damn him.

My finger jabs the phone icon. I pull up his number and hit dial. The phone rings three times before dropping me into voice mail.

"Leave a message." Smythe's recorded voice requests.

Happy to oblige.

"Smythe, it's Gin. Again. We need to talk. Did you get my other message? Did you hear you left me to deal with a demon on my own? On. My. Own. What kind of mentor leaves his *Justitian* to deal with a demon ON HER OWN?" I draw in a breath, pulling my shrill voice back to a normal tone. "You need to call me. We need to talk. You hear? Call me. Or pick up my calls."

I yank the phone away from my ear, stabbing the end button like it's a demon. Like how I should've killed Rahab last night.

Like I killed Donny.

My knees give out as I collapse upon the bed. Anger spent, sadness swamps me like a tidal wave of anguish.

I killed Donny.

"Gin?" T yells. "Dinner's ready. You finished reaming Smythe a new one?"

I swallow, dash the tears away from my eyes and clear my throat. "Yeah. Be there in a second."

Dropping the phone on the nightstand, I drag my feet to the door. No use in appearing anything other than what I feel. T reads me like a book. A perk of being twins I never minded before.

Now I want to be left alone to deal with my grief.

No such luck.

Chapter Three

The weekend drags. Smythe continues to ignore my calls. T continues to baby me. Grief continues to assault me. Monday morning finds me red-eyed from too many thoughts and not enough sleep. Despite my lack of a good night's rest, I manage to haul my ass into work early and not so bright, due to the morning sun hovering at the horizon. A dull ache in my chest continues to remind me of my losses.

Perhaps a day in the Emergency Department will give me some relief from the unending pain.

After locking my purse in my locker, I report to the nurses' station for a debriefing. Jon, the night nurse, shakes his head when I ask for a status update. Never a good sign.

"You want the good, the bad, or the ugly first?"

Yep. Definite bad sign. And it's not even a full moon.

"Start with the good." I need something uplifting.

"All right." He leans forward, tired brown eyes focusing on my face. "Mr. Ripley in room one came in with fever, cough, and shortness of breath. Come to find out, he has pneumonia and they're admitting him for IV antibiotics."

"And he's the good one?"

"Oh yeah." He pushes back in his chair, shaking his head. "It's been crazy."

I glance around the calm ER, the only noises the beeps of machines and the whirl of the HVAC system. "Sounds quiet to me."

"Because the dead don't speak."

Unless you're T. They'll speak to my twin. A tidbit I keep to myself.

"What happened?"

He clears his throat, the tiredness in his gaze morphing into a conspiratory glee, as if patient gossip gives him a high. "It started Friday evening. Maybe you saw this one on the news? The Dallas Baptist deacon who committed suicide?"

"Unfortunately, yeah."

"The others aren't high profile, so didn't make the news. At least not that I know of. But there were several suicides on Saturday and five more came in last night. And that was just at our hospital. Other hospitals experienced the same thing. And not a one of the dead were depressed. At least not according to family members. It's like demons possessed them or something."

I blink. Demons? The word jerks me back to the dream man sitting on my toilet lid. The man T claimed was real. The man I insisted was a dream.

A dream man who offered me relief from my troubles.

What if the man wasn't a dream? What if it was really a demon? But if that was the case, wouldn't my *justitia* have turned into a demon-killing sword?

"Gin?" Jon snaps his fingers in front of my nose.

I blink. Good way to look inconspicuous, Gin. "Sorry. Was just thinking of those poor families. It's horrible."

"Yeah. All those suicides were the bad part of the evening."

"You mean there's more?"

"I'm telling you, it was like the whole city went psycho or something. There was also this hideous car wreck. No survivors. The bodies? That was the ugly." He stands, shoving his chair under the desk. "Well, I'm off. Enjoy the crazy ER."

Jon raps his knuckles twice on the desk and strides to the break room, clearly eager to get the hell out of here.

I don't blame him. After an evening like he described, I kinda want to leave too.

No such luck. The little thing called "bills" keeps me chained to this place.

By the time seven in the evening rolls around, I'm exhausted, emotionally drained, and still thinking of how I screwed up at Club Monster. So much for leaving my worries at the door. Perhaps it had to do with the number of suicides along with their distraught family members.

The good thing is we only had two more suicides today, if that could be called good. Definitely an improvement over last night but zero would have been better. Unless the city of Dallas decided to waft some sort of a "kill me now" drug through the air, the sheer volume of suicides in a single day lent credence to demonic involvement.

Which means I need to drag my tired and drained ass out to patrol the streets and see what I can find.

Although how I'm supposed to hunt without a guardian mage is beyond me.

Instead, I clock out and drive home.

Once the garage door closes behind me, I yank my phone out of my purse and place yet another call to my missing mentor.

Why am I not surprised the call drops into voice mail?

"Look here, Smythe. You are acting like a PMS'ing woman. Okay, whatever. That's your biz, but there is something going on in Dallas. There've been a ton of suicides since Friday night and that's not normal. I suspect demonic involvement. You should too. So get over yourself, man up, and call me back. You can be as mad at me as you want but you need to do your job and get your ass to my place so we can hunt down whatever is causing this epidemic. Okay? Bye."

If my voice mail doesn't get a response, I'm calling the Agency hotline and requesting another mentor. The thought of which causes the low-level ache in my chest to bloom into a full-blown maybe-I'm-having-a-heart-attack sensation. I don't want it to be over between us. I want Smythe to remain as my mentor. And my lover, although getting him back is looking less likely by the second. Even if he never crawls into my bed again, I still want to work with him.

I also want to kick his ass around the block for leaving me alone to handle a fight with a demon.

For ignoring my calls.

Jackass.

As soon as I step into the kitchen, T yells from the living room.

"Hey! I cooked you dinner."

I stand by the door blinking for a two count. Who or what replaced my brother with a cook?

"Are you okay?" I set my purse on the table and

head toward T, stopping in the doorway between the kitchen and the living room.

"Yeah, why?"

"I'm not trying to be ungrateful, but since when do you cook me dinner?"

He shrugs, turns back to the baseball game on TV. "I was hungry so I cooked you some too."

I don't need to read his mind to know he's worried about me. Cooking dinner is his way of trying to make me feel better. For the first time in a while, a smile crosses my lips.

"I appreciate it. Not trying to be a bitch."

"I know." He looks at me, one side of his mouth turning in a crooked grin. "Your plate is in the microwave."

I open the microwave to find a plate containing a grilled steak, grilled asparagus, and formerly frozen steak fries. Yummy.

"I'm going to change, then I'll be right in."

A few minutes later I'm back in the kitchen dressed in a pair of PJs and house slippers. After nuking my plate, I march it and myself into the living room, kick off my slippers and flop on the couch beside my brother, the awesome cook.

"How was your day?" I stuff a fry into my mouth, talking around it.

"Same ol', same ol'. You?"

I chew a bite while he curses at the TV when his player strikes out. Once he eases back onto the couch, I speak.

"Bunch of suicides. I suspect a demon."

"Ah, shit. Don't tell me you have to go hunt it?"

My ringing phone postpones our usual argument. I

glance at the caller ID. "Hang on."

I set my plate on the coffee table and run-walk to the kitchen, swiping the talk button.

"Hello?"

"You're right." The tight tone of Smythe's voice lets me know he's not happy about the matter. "Despite the Agency not reporting any demon appearances, the likelihood of a demon outbreak in Dallas is high. The number of suicides is abnormal. I checked."

"Nice to talk to you too. So what are we going to do about it?" About the demon. About the suicides. About us. Pick one.

Of course he avoids the tutu-wearing elephant sitting between us, choosing the safer territory of demons. Then again, I asked about the demon and suicides, not us.

"You working tomorrow?"

"Not tomorrow. But I am the next day."

"I'll be at your house at seven in the morning. Be ready to go."

With those words, he ends the call.

Not a bad start. At least he talked. More like growled. Beggars can't be choosers, can they?

"Who was that?" T asks as I walk back to the couch.

I pick up my plate and cram a bite of steak into my mouth. "Smythe."

"Son of a bitch. Did you let him play all nicey-nicey?"

"It wasn't like that."

"Aw man," he points at the TV with his beer bottle, "did you see what just happened? Rogers struck out. Damn it. So, what was it like?"

"Smythe or the strike out?"

"We're talking about your mentor."

"Right." I swallow, replacing the piece of steak with a fry. "He apparently listened to my latest voice mail and decided I had a point about the suicides being demon involvement. He's coming over tomorrow morning."

"Damn. I don't like it."

"We've been over this before."

"I still don't like it. Why did the bracelet have to pick you?"

"Jealous?"

He snorts. "Right. Couldn't it have picked someone else?"

"There is no one else. I'm the last of the line."

"So Smythe's coming over in the morning. Whatcha going to do about him being an ass?" T takes a sip of beer, peering at me as he swallows.

I shrug. "Don't know yet."

"Want me to talk him?"

Oh, like that would go over well. "Thanks, but no thanks."

"It's not a problem."

"It's appreciated, but no. I can handle him on my own."

"Give him hell before you forgive him."

"Who says I'll forgive him?"

T takes a sip. "Uh-huh."

"I thought you took his side."

"Haven't you heard of the Devil's advocate?"

I roll my eyes. "Thanks."

"Any time sis, any time." He pats my arm with one hand, jostling my plate.

"Thanks again for dinner."

"Don't mention it."

When I slip into my bedroom hours later to go to bed—after our team wins and the kitchen is clean—I glance in the corners, half expecting Zagan to appear. No such luck. Until faced with a room empty of all but the furniture, I never realized how much the demon meant to me. In some twisted way, we've become friends.

Gah. Did I actually have that thought?

A dull shake from my bracelet confirms I did. And the entity in the thing agrees.

Double *gah.*

Not sure what it says about me when I miss a demon lurking in the shadows of my room.

Pain throbs in my chest. Zagan called me worthless. A loser. Despite my kickass skills in the ER, my skills to rid the world of demons clearly sucks. Along with the ability to keep a man and avoid killing humans.

It's a sad day when a demon makes a good point about your personality.

A sharp sting pierces my wrist as the silver links of the *justitia* shake against skin. Memories flit through my mind, too fast to see, the speed causing a dizzy spell.

Closing my eyes, I slide down the closed door, until my butt hits the floor. The memories slow, settle, focus on an ancient scene. Zagan playing blacksmith, hammering a mass of silver, sweat beading across his brow. The scene changes to him linking small silver plates into bracelets. Thirteen bracelets. Thirteen bracelets that look a lot like the thirteen *justitias* worn by my fellow sword-sisters.

Not look like, *are*. I know this as sure as I know my name. I'm watching the beginnings of the bracelets.

The scene shifts again. This time thirteen multihued demons stand in a circle around a fire, each clutching a bracelet in their clawed hands. Before each demon stands a small, gnome-like creature, minus the typical pointed hats. Human cries for help, wails of terror and fear, sound in the background, close but hidden in shadows. The stench of sulfur hangs in the air, a pleasing scent of home. The scene appears as if I'm looking out of one of the gnome-like creatures' eyes.

The demons start chanting, wicked words flowing in a spine-tingling rhythm, a forceful spell brushing against my—the gnome creature's—skin.

Freely given blood of servants, blood of power
Silver strong, others will cower
Weld the two, strength doubled into one
Form an entity stoppable by none
With the links, the weak will be made strong
Let them strive to right a wrong
When we complete this spell
We will be rulers of Hell

Firelight flashes off silver knives as the demons slash their palms. Black blood drips onto the dirt floor, the sweet scent of copper and sulfur filling the air. Fear and anticipation ripple through my veins as the demons smear their blood over the silver links of the bracelets. The crackle of magic shakes my marrow as the spell takes hold.

Excitement turns into shock as each demon slits the throat of my fellow servants before them, as the sharp sting of a knife slices through my own throat. A shot of panic ricochets through my limbs as I fight not to struggle. My knees give out and I fall onto the ground, hands clasped against my severed neck, my blood a spreading crimson stain on the dirt.

Pain fills my body as blood spills onto the ground, as my life pumps toward death. But it is only death of the body. Because of the spell, my soul streams into the silver bracelet, joins the metal, merges into one being.

My new home is tight, small, binding. I am, and yet, I cannot move. I see, and yet I no longer reside in a body. My body, limp and lifeless, a vessel no longer needed.

The touch of a finger stroking the metal links of the bracelet, of me, halts the budding panic. Zagan holds me, no, no longer my body, but the bracelet. I am a silver linked bracelet. I am changed.

"Hello, lovely. You did good. Just a little longer."

I settle at his words, at the kindness in his voice. He means so much to me. I'd do anything for him. Anything. I am his faithful servant. He needs my help. Only I can help my master. Yes, there are others like me, twelve others, but they do not serve my master. They serve their masters. My master is better. My master has a plan.

And I am created to help him achieve it.

Human females are brought forward, their annoying cries echoing through the chamber, tears soaking their cheeks. Fear creases their faces, stinks their sweat. They fear my master. I reveal in the pleasure he derives from their sobs.

He selects the largest female, the one standing in the front, her eyes flashing a warning despite her fear.

The strongest. The one best suited for his purpose. He drags her resisting body into a circle drawn onto the floor. She tries to run, the spell powering the circle stopping her short. Only demons can pass through the circle; humans stand caught by the magic within.

One by one, each demon selects the female who shall wear their bracelet, dragging the woman into the middle of the circle. Chosen prior to the ritual, our female knows not how special she is, knows not why she was selected.

The demons stay on the outside of the circle, whispered words drawing their chosen female to stand before them, captivated, quiet, unable to resist. Tension runs through my master's fingers into my new body as he clutches me in his palm.

He glances around the circle, eyeing each demon-female pair, ensuring all is in order. The chamber fills with the crackle of burning oak. One minute passes, then another, as each demon prepares to perform the difficult spell.

My master lifts his hand, dropping it in a slashing motion. The signal to begin. Again, the demons chant. Blue and purple tendrils wrap me and the female in magic, draw us together, bind our souls. The female's eyes widen. Even through the compulsion laid upon her, she senses the change, knows she is powerless to stop the spell from joining her body to my soul. Energy fills the air, fills the female, fills my soul. I am one. I am chosen. I am needed.

My silver links surround the thin wrist of human flesh, clasp and seal shut. The spell binds us, transforming our separate destinies into one. I feel her trembling pulse race against me. Sense her nerves tingling beneath my metal. I take my place along her nerves, throughout her body, binding us together, holding her to the demon through me. I race through her body until I find her mind.

Her scared mind.

Then I introduce myself.

And nothing will ever be the same.

****

With a gasp, my lids fly open. A quick glance at my arms proves I am Gin, not some freshly-killed gnome creature in a chamber full of spell-chanting demons. I sit on the floor of my bedroom, alone with the light and the air conditioner rattling the vent. My limbs tremble as if dunked in freezing water.

A dream? A memory? What the hell? If the *justitia* can show me memories that vivid, why can't it answer my questions? Like how the heck it hopped from Will's scrub pocket into mine?

Laughter trails along my nerves, courtesy of the *justitia. You see. You know. You are me.*

My *justitia* talks! Before, I'd gotten glimpses of its past along with short one-word responses, but full sentences never seemed within its abilities. Until now. I close my eyes, focusing on the purple light of the entity along my nerves.

You were killed to create my justitia. *Why?*

A long pause, then an eerie voice sounds in my mind.

My master needed power.

Okay. Finally. I'm having a conversation, in the loosest sense of the word, with my *justitia.*

Zagan was your master, right?

Sparks of purple drift through my mind as the

entity answers. *Yes. Good master.*

If you belonged to Zagan, how did you end up at the Agency? What happened to the woman who first wore you?

Scenes flash through my mind, swirling, circling, a plug pulled on a drain. A gray mist fuzzes the scenes, obliterating the memory.

No.

My eyes pop open in surprise, but I quickly shut them to concentrate on our conversation. *No? What do you mean, no?*

Not yet. Not ready. Soon.

So much for talking with my *justitia*. But at least I learned some things. Which is more than the esteemed Agency taught me. If the demons created the *justitias*, then how did they fall into Agency hands? How could a demonic spell be broken? And why? More importantly, if the demons created the bracelets, why do the bracelets now kill their creators?

With a wheeze, the AC cuts off, but chills continue to wrack my limbs. Chills of knowledge. Chills of shock. Sometimes ignorance really is bliss.

Chapter Four

A buzzing alarm yanks me from a dark dream, memories scattering into oblivion as I open my eyes. Unease creeps across my skin as I slap a hand on the alarm's off button. Six o'clock? Why am I up so early on my day off?

The reason pops to the front of my mind. Smythe. Here. At 7:00 a.m. I need enough caffeine in me by the time he arrives to make sense and not be grumpy.

Wait. A little grumpy might be needed. I might want to work with him but I sure as hell am not ready to forgive him.

Not yet anyway.

Twenty minutes later I walk into the kitchen, following the scent of fresh-brewed coffee. T stands at the counter dressed in black trousers and his gray auto shop work shirt, watching the pot do its drip-drip thing.

"Hey." At my voice, he turns, one brow raised.

"Whatcha doing up so early? Aren't you off?"

"Smythe's coming over."

His jaw clenches. "Right. I forgot."

I pull the cereal box out of the pantry, dumping the off-brand shredded wheat into a bowl. "We're going to discuss the possible demon activity, remember?"

"Then you're gonna chew out his ass, right?"

"Maybe." I shrug.

"Maybe? No maybe about it. The man's behaving

34

like a jerk."

Now it's my turn for a raised brow. "Thought you understood why he wouldn't return my calls."

"Sure, but it's my sister who's upset, so he's being a jerk."

I smile. "I like your reasoning."

He pours a cup of coffee, pulls out my extra-large mug and fills it with the wonderful black liquid.

I take a sip. "Mmm. Thanks."

"Never say I don't understand you."

I point the mug at him. "Never say I don't understand *you*."

One corner of his mouth turns up. He doesn't need to say it, I know what sparks through his mind.

I hold his gaze for a moment longer, a silent way of saying how glad I am to have him as my brother.

He yanks the cereal box out of my hand, gives the opening a sniff followed by a nose wrinkle. "Don't know how you can eat this stuff."

"It's not so bad." I take my bowl, spoon, and mug to the table, T following with his mug and the box of sugary bad-for-you cereal he loves.

By the time we finish eating, the coffee has worked a miracle, firing my brain cells into action. I pour another cup and open the paper, sipping as I read. The feel of the paper, the smell of the ink, usually puts me in my happy place. Sure, I could pull up the paper on my phone, but reading digitally isn't quite the same experience.

Call me old fashioned.

Two-thirds of the way through the paper, a portal forms in my kitchen, deceptively warm air gushing into the room. Smythe steps out, dressed in a navy blue long-sleeved shirt and jeans, his black laptop backpack thrown over one shoulder. At six-foot-five with short black hair and blue eyes, he commands attention.

And despite his current asshat behavior, an invisible pull focuses my gaze on him to the extent everything else in the room fades away.

I swear my heart stops along with my breath. Smythe's gaze hits me with the force of a tsunami, drowning me in its depths, its regrets, its anger. The silent communication of longing and ire between Smythe and me breaks when T turns to see why I'm staring over his shoulder. With a thud, my heart resumes a staccato beat and I suck in a shaky breath. T stiffens. Tension flows through the room, thick as spilled sewage.

But my twin's strained posture isn't nearly as bad as my mentor's. Smythe resembles a cross between a man sucking on a persimmon and a glowering thunderhead. As if he can't decide between being pissed off or bitter. Neither of which bodes well for me.

But since he and T play the stare-and-glare game, I decide to be nice and start our long overdue conversation.

"Hey. Thanks for coming."

Smythe's eyes narrow, focusing on me again instead of my twin. "Still drinking coffee, I see."

His tone is a cross between humor and annoyance, as if I should be ashamed for drinking so much coffee.

I'm not. Shame fail.

I shrug, forcing my hands to unclench. "It's better than other things."

Before Smythe can answer, T shoves back his chair, the legs squeaking across the floor, and points a finger at Smythe.

I hop to my feet, ready to throw myself between the two and save T from being annihilated. My twin might be a badass, but Smythe has a little something called magic on his side.

"Listen, asshat," T drops his finger as he moves to stand nose to chin with Smythe. "You hurt my sister again and mage or not, you'll have me to deal with."

Smythe's jaw tenses. His fingers flex. He stares at T long enough for the temperature in the room to drop a few degrees. I rub my goosebump-covered arms, wondering if I should intervene. Right when I'm about to put my life at risk by coming between the two, T takes a step back. Smythe continues to stare at my twin, his eyes the shade of glacial ice.

T seems to grow, his aura expanding until the room warms, the earlier chill evaporating under the onslaught of his rage. Maybe I was wrong. Maybe T could take on Smythe and win. After another couple of stare-and-glare seconds, T turns his back on Smythe in an either brave or foolhardy move. A moment later his arms wrap around me, holding me close.

Don't worry about him, Gin, he got the message. See you tonight.

I return his hug, breathing in a deep, relieved breath. *Thank you. But don't do it again. I don't want him to hurt you.*

T snorts. *Like he could.*

But—

No buts about it. I'm fine. Make sure you've kicked his ass to Oklahoma by the time I get back.

I bite off a chuckle. *If you insist.*

He gives me a peck on the cheek. "See ya later."

"Have fun at work."

On his way to the front door, T bumps into Smythe shoulder-to-shoulder, the male equivalent of *don't mess with me, bitch.*

Smythe turns with his fists clenched, his gaze following T's exit. He blows out a heavy breath when the door closes behind my twin and crosses his arms.

"Your brother has an anger problem."

And in under a second, I go from wary and concerned to hot-cheeked bitchzilla. Want to see anger, buster? Just watch. "Oh? *He* has an anger problem? He's not the one who's been ignoring my calls. Who left me alone to deal with a demon. Who—"

His eyes snap blue fire. "We don't have time for your tirade. You made your choice—"

"Are you freaking kidding me?" I take a step toward him, my voice rising an octave. "Have you not read the papers? Did the cleanup crew not report back to you? Donny is dead!"

Smythe jerks as if slapped. "Dead? When did that happen?"

"Geez, Smythe! Have you not seen the news?"

He rolls his hand in a circular motion, Smythe talk for nope so get on with it.

I draw in a deep breath, trying to return my voice to a normal, non-screeching level. So much for that attempt. At least when my jaw clenches, I don't sound so shrill. "When you misread the situation at the club and stormed out, Rahab stormed in, before I could chase after you. You left me to deal with a demon and his minion. You left me." So much for not sounding shrill. I'm surprised the light bulb remains in one piece after I shrieked that last sentence.

"You kissed him." The growling undertone of his voice holds betrayal and hurt, along with a good deal of jealousy and ire.

I'm not swayed.

"Grow eyes! He planted one on me. You walked in right as I was about to kick him in the nuts. And then left without letting me explain." Does Smythe really think *I* kissed Donny?

Smythe blinks twice, red dotting his cheeks, his eyes gleaming with barely concealed ire. "I don't want to discuss this right now. I came to hunt demons."

"What do you mean, you don't want to discuss it?" My breath comes in small bursts, pained and uneven, as my voice lowers to a level usually indicative of an impending thunderstorm. My fists clench. I swear my head is about to explode.

He draws in a noisy breath through his nose. "I mean, not now. I don't want to deal with this now." His pained gaze implores me to shut the hell up.

Yeah, right. As if that's going to happen.

"You had to know this would come up. We need—"

"What we need to do is hunt this demon. Then maybe we can discuss what went on."

Maybe? Maybe? The man is nuts if he thinks maybe is an option. Definitely is more like it.

I swallow the thought. I'm not ready to forgive him. Yell at him, yes. Make him hurt like he made me hurt, sure. But forgive him? Not yet. And standing in front of him, I realize he feels the same. He thinks, truly thinks, I owe *him* an apology. He mistakenly believes *I* betrayed *him*. That it's *me* who needs to ask for forgiveness.

He is so freaking wrong, I don't even know where to start.

So I do as he asks, shove the anger aside and focus on the demon problem. Or try to shove the anger aside. I really, really, really want to slap him upside the head.

More than once.

Deep breaths, Gin, deep breaths.

My chest aches, my head pounds with the rhythm of my speeding heart, but I manage to unclench my fists while attempting to speak in a normal, not-going-to-kill-you voice.

"I'm pretty sure a demon is behind all these suicides. That's why I asked you to come." See, I can talk in a normal tone while suppressing homicidal tendencies.

Despite this accomplishment, hot tears press against my eyes. Damn it. No way am I going to cry in front of him.

"I agree." Smythe slows his speech, as if dragging out his words helps keep him calm. "Several demons feed off suicides. The most prominent ones are the despair demons, but I've never known them to cause suicidal tendencies. They show up once the deed has been done."

The memory of lying in the bathtub, hungover and depressed while some dream man beckoned me to him, flashes to the front of my mind. He called me. He wanted me. If not for T, he would have taken me. Goosebumps snake across my skin. I cross my arms in a failed attempt not to shake.

"Maybe something changed. Maybe it's not the normal herd of demons feeding off the depressed. Maybe there's one who urges a depressed person to come to them. Maybe that demon's hungry."

Smythe raises a brow. "Let's say you're right. Why now?"

"And which demon?"

He places his backpack on the floor and leans against the wall while he talks. "We already covered it. One of the despair demons."

"Yeah, I know, but which one? Do they have leaders? Like groups or something?"

His look lets me know he thinks I'm one sandwich short of a picnic. "Of course. For instance, you fought Agramon, the fear demon."

A shiver courses through me at the mention of the demon's name, a cold remembrance of almost dying. Agramon was one scary-ass demon, the likes of which I hope to never see again.

"He was the leader of all fear demons."

"You mean there are more of them?" My breath hitches. *Please say no.*

Turns out, I'm disappointed.

"Yep. You killed the leader, which means another, less powerful fear demon now leads them."

My *justitia* jiggles. It feared Agramon almost as much as I did. Something tickles my memory, a distant fog obscuring the landscape. What was it? What about Agramon's death brought an ancient memory of the *justitia* bubbling to the surface?

The *justitia's* memory appears in my mind. Multi-hued demons stand around a fire, lips turned in macabre grins as they stare at weeping women draping the ground before them.

And now I shall rule all. Zagan's voice zips through my mind, my *justitia*'s memory, threat and desire rolled into one.

But what does the bracelets' beginning have to do with Agramon's death?

"Gin?"

I startle at the sound of Smythe's voice, blinking a couple of times for good measure. He shoots me a worried look rimmed with anger.

"Sorry. You ever have a memory try to come out of hiding but not make it?"

"Yeah. Let me know when you think of it."

I nod, resuming our conversation prior to my trip down the *justitia's* memory lane. "I hope never to see another fear demon again. Ever. Agramon was one scary mother."

Smythe cracks a grin. "Yep. But you killed him." His eyes narrow, grin fading. "With Zagan's help."

I cross my arms at the jab as I remember using red energy given to me by Zagan to kill the fear demon. "I'll take all the help I can get."

"And therein lies your problem, Gin."

A spike of anger floods my system. I draw in a deep breath. Okay, I get it. He was raised with the belief demons are slimebags who should never be talked to or trusted. Anyone who disobeys those rules has a problem.

Just because I understand him doesn't mean I have to like him judging me. I'm not the only one with issues. For once my reasoning fails to make me feel better.

"Yeah? Well, at least I killed the thing. The other *Justitians* who wore my bracelet and fought Agramon lost."

"Because they didn't let a demon give them special

powers. None of them allowed a demon to fill them with its energy." Low and ominous, the tone of his voice rolls across my skin.

"Don't worry, Smythe. Zagan's pissed at me too so I no longer have those special powers. I'm back to being plain ol' me."

Which bothers me way more than it should. I should be grateful Zagan, the demon of deceit, no longer wants me around. Instead, his absence is yet another thing making me tear up.

I will not cry, I will not cry, I will not cry.

The tears vanish, but the ache in my chest is an empty cave of sorrow threatening to smother me. Part of me wants to crawl under my bed, curl in the fetal position, and hide from the world.

Whispered words fill my mind. *Come to me. I will give you rest.*

Is the whispering voice in my head a return of the dream man or a memory?

Strong hands wrap around my upper arms, give me a shake. I blink several times. Smythe stands in front of me, a line curving his brow, his features stamped with concern. How could I not realize he moved?

"What just happened, Gin?"

"Nothing. Just lost in space." Like I'm going to tell him about the dream man, who may or may not be real.

My *justitia* shakes, as a warning or trying to give advice?

"Bullshit. You got a distant expression on your face and then something was in your mind."

Straightening my coffee mug before the liquid gold spills to a wasted puddle on the floor, I ignore how his warm hands still grip my arms, how his closeness wraps me in warmth, how his concern touches me. Yeah, none of those things matter. What the hell does he mean something was in my mind? T said the same thing when he found me in the bathtub, hungover and wanting to die.

To die. Like the suicides.

No way. Could there be a connection? Nausea roils through my suddenly freezing body.

"What do you mean, something was in my mind? What were you doing in my mind?"

He ignores the second question, focusing on the first, more important question.

"Something was definitely in your mind. Like a spirit or something. I've never felt anything like it. You aren't possessed—"

"How can you tell?" I don't think I'm possessed, but the more I know, the smarter a demon huntress I'll be.

And, in theory, the better I'll be at fighting the dream man. Fight him I will. I don't want what he's offering.

Really. I don't.

Lying has always been my forte.

Unaware of my internal dialogue, Smythe answers my question. "You'd have another aura shadowing yours. A black or gray one. You don't. But something was there, talking to you. I didn't catch what it said."

"Come to me, I'll give you rest. Those are its words." I swallow, trying to rid my throat of its sudden dryness.

"Who?"

"Don't know." Should I tell him about the dream man? I take a breath. Yes, I should. Hearing strange voices is not a route I wish to travel. Maybe he can help. "I first heard him the other day. After"—I swallow—"after I killed Donny. The next morning. I was"—yeah, not going there about how effed-up I was—"um, I was taking a bath, and it was like I was in a dream world. There was this man sitting on my toilet lid and he reached out a hand and told me to come to him. Said he could give me peace. Then T stormed in because, like you, he heard the man in my head. The man disappeared." I snap my fingers. "Poof. Gone. Clearly a disturbing waking dream."

"And your *justitia* didn't do anything?" He slides his hand down my arm to finger the silver links.

Right. He's still standing close to me, close enough to kiss. Like that's going to happen.

I glance at his hand, then to his eyes, then back to his hand. He drops his grip and takes a step back, light red tingeing his cheeks.

"No. Which means this can't be a demon, right? I thought it might be, when T said he could hear the voice in my mind, but the *justitia* would turn into a sword, right?" Relief sweeps through me. Not a demon. Although it presented a problem. If not a demon and not a dream, then what was the man in my mind?

"If the demon appeared in front of you, then yes, the *justitia* would morph into a sword."

"Sounds like there's a 'but' in there."

"No 'but'; just a thought."

He pauses, forehead furrowed into deep thought lines.

"Go on."

"What if the demon can project himself to you? The *justitia* must have a demon in its sights. The distance varies from *justitia* to *justitia* so it's possible a demon could be a couple of houses over and the *justitia* not turn. If a demon can project itself to a victim, then it could be hiding anywhere and not be picked up by the *justitia.*"

Oh great. Something far scarier than Agramon. A demon projecting himself to victims. So much for the sense of relief. My skin prickles into goosebumps. I take a sip of lukewarm coffee to try to warm up.

No such luck.

"That's damn scary."

"Yeah. I'll do some research when we get back from demon hunting."

"While you're at it, why don't you tell me what you were doing in my mind."

His lips flatten. "I wasn't in your mind. Not at first. I felt a presence inside you. It was easy to hop in; your defenses were down."

Heat slaps my cheeks. The last thing I want is for him to know how awful I felt, still feel. I want to project a tough image. I don't want him to forgive me because he pities me. I'm not ready to show a soft side with Smythe. One day, but not now. The pain is too fresh, too much of a never-ending ache to share with one of its main causes.

Which means I need to pretend like there's only one thing on my mind.

I place the mug on the counter. "Let's go hunt a demon."

Chapter Five

Smythe portals us to the first victim's house, the Sunday school teacher, a deacon in the large, downtown Baptist church. We land along the side of a house two doors down, hidden behind an overgrown photinia bush. My heels sink into the soft dirt. Why, oh why, did I decide to look business casual by wearing slacks and nice shoes? Now I have to clean the muddy things.

My professional look marred by dirt.

Once we step onto the sidewalk, Smythe flicks a finger at my shoes, removing the dirt and saving me from a muddy cleaning job.

Maybe he's not so bad after all.

Which doesn't make me any less mad at him.

Smythe strides to the door and rings the bell. A couple of seconds later, the creak of footsteps against hardwood floors draws closer. A middle-aged, average height woman with red-rimmed eyes and a fading bruise on one cheek opens the door. Her short brown hair sticks out in different directions.

"Janet Luckey?"

"Yes?"

Smythe pulls out his magic badge, flips it open and closed and the woman's eyes glaze. An absurd thought pops into my head as I watch her fall under his Agent-Smythe-and-Consultant-Crawford spell. Does she see him in a typical FBI suit and tie, or does she seem him dressed as he is in jeans and a long-sleeved navy shirt?

The only time I've ever seen Smythe in a suit—albeit one minus the tie—was the first night he took me to Club Monster to see if a demon used the club as a hidey-hole. Memories tumble faster than I can bring them into focus—Smythe and me in bed, me fighting Rahab and killing Donny instead, Smythe walking out mad, Zagan calling me worthless—each leaving behind an impression of loss, of emptiness.

An invisible hand reaches inside my chest, squeezes my heart until my breath catches, until tears spring to my eyes.

Depression, an overwhelming sadness, surrounds me, burrows deep inside.

Come to me.

The voice floats through my mind as Smythe introduces us as our fake FBI personas.

The woman steps back, holding the door for us to enter, but Smythe grabs my wrist, touching my *justitia*. A jolt of white light rockets through me, exorcising the voice from my mind, leaving me reeling.

Good thing Smythe takes a grip on my elbow. Falling on the floor while on a mission would be embarrassing. More so than crying in front of Smythe. Luckily the streak of white light banishes the tears.

For now.

"What does the FBI want with my husband's death?" Mrs. Luckey asks, gesturing us to sit on the couch.

I plop onto the overstuffed sofa sinking into its depths. How the hell people can get comfy on these things is over my head. I scoot forward, trying to get comfortable without seeming obvious while Smythe sits next to me, upright and all business. Mrs. Luckey lowers herself into a chair next to the couch, worry and exhaustion written into the lines on her face.

"Your husband was the first of several suicides since Friday. We're investigating the cause. Was he taking any new medication?" Smythe uses his soothing, open-up-and-talk-to-me voice, the one that lulls an unsuspecting person into spilling their guts.

She shakes her head. "No, not that I'm aware of. I looked."

"Any strange behavior the day of his passing?"

Her eyes widen before she looks at her hands clutched together in her lap. She shakes her head.

"Mrs. Luckey." I look at her until she glances up at me. "How did you get your bruise?" I point to my own eye as tears well in hers.

"He went nuts," she whispers, as if mentioning this fact aloud will send her straight to Hell. "Nuts." She clears her throat, voice strengthening as she talks. "He was in his office," she points down the hall. Smythe looks, but I keep my gaze on her.

"Yelling to leave him alone. Over and over. But no one was in the house except me. After about three or four times, I went to see what was wrong. And he hit me!" Her palm rests against her bruised cheek, surprise flitting through her eyes.

"I take it that never happened before?"

She looks at Smythe, eyes narrowing to make a point of defense for her husband's character. "Never. He was a good man. He'd never hit me. When he saw it was me, he stopped yelling, his eyes big as a serving platter. He said he was sorry, so, so sorry, then he ran out of the room. I thought he was going to get ice or something, but the next thing I hear is a gun firing." Her breath hitches as tears stream down her face. "Please excuse me."

Leaving us sitting in the living room, she walks into the kitchen to grab a tissue. Smythe drums the fingers of one hand against his leg, rolling them pinky to thumb, pinky to thumb. He draws in a breath before she makes it back to her chair. I interrupt whatever speech he plans.

"I'm so sorry, Mrs. Luckey. I know this is hard for you."

"Thank you." She nods. "I never expected..." her voice trails away as she gestures her hand toward the hall.

"Had anything happened this week to upset your husband?"

"Not that I'm aware of. He seemed happy and normal at dinner. Then, he just went nuts when he got to his office. He was working on his Sunday lesson."

"May we look in his office?"

She nods, a puzzled look crossing her face. "Wouldn't you rather see where he shot himself?"

"I'm sure the police have thoroughly covered it. We'd rather look at his office."

"This way. But I warn you, it's a mess. I haven't been able to bring myself to clean it." She leads us down a short hall to a room on the right. One hand points at the room. "He did all his church lessons in there."

The deacon's office holds book shelves along the walls, a desk with a computer, two chairs and enough papers scattered around to keep a maid busy for a month. No wonder she hasn't cleaned it. The task would be daunting enough if she were the maid and not the grieving wife of the deceased.

"Can you let us into the computer?" An undercurrent of glee at the prospect of looking into the deacon's files edges through Smythe's voice. Hopefully Mrs. Luckey doesn't hear it.

"It's not password protected." She waves a hand at the machine while giving a little shrug. "Help yourself. Do you need me to watch?"

Smythe shakes his head. "I'd prefer you didn't."

"Okay. I'll be in the kitchen. Want something to drink?"

"No, thank you."

She's no sooner taken two steps down the hall than Smythe has accessed the computer. I activate the minion sensors in my eyes, looking for red or orange trails left behind as evidence of a minion presence, but nothing out of the ordinary appears. Unless one considers the copious amount of paper spread over every surface.

"No minions."

"I didn't see any evidence either." Smythe taps on the keyboard, staring at the screen.

Mages can see minion trails as well as *Justitians*. Which begs the question of why they don't take our bracelets and fight the demonic hellions themselves.

Only you can wear us, my *justitia* chants in my head. *You are special. Mage is not.*

While I'm not surprised at the truth it speaks, it continues to surprise, and please, me by speaking in my mind. Until the other day, the thing limited its communications to memory fragments and one-word responses.

Me like you. Me say more.

Great. Then why don't you start by telling me where you disappeared after my ancestral line died out and if the line was dead, how did I get to wear you?

No response, except for the impression of a shrug, as if it's a teenager refusing to talk. So much for a conversation.

One of these days, I'm going to learn the answer. My ancestral line died when the last *Justitian* who wore my bracelet tried to kill Hitler. We all knew he was evil, the fact he was a minion comes as no surprise. What is a surprise? My ability to wear a *justitia* from a dead ancestral line.

I grab a stack of papers, intending to sit in one of the chairs. My gaze focuses on the scrawled handwriting. Someone clearly made a F in handwriting class. I squint, trying to read the almost indecipherable writing. When I finally make it out, my breath hitches. I pick up another piece of paper, then another one.

"Smythe?"

"What?" He continues to stare at the computer as his fingers *tap-tap-tap* against the keys.

"Look at this." I hold a piece of paper out to him. "Every page is the same."

Smythe pauses, grabs the paper, his eyes widening as he reads.

Get away from me Satan is written over and over on each page, the scrawled writing a glimpse into a distraught mind.

Smythe lets loose a low whistle. "What do you think he saw? It wasn't a demon; I checked before I came. At least not one the Agency's demon identification program picked up."

I suppress an eye roll. The program is about as accurate as a meteorologist's forecast. "We all know how correct the thing is."

He raises a brow, otherwise ignoring my snarky remark. "As I was saying, no one was in the house except his wife. No minion. No demon. So what did he see? And why?"

"No clue. But something was definitely going on with him." *Good job stating the obvious, Gin.*

Smythe pauses, gathering his thoughts or wishing I would gather mine? "We need to know why he was targeted. Why they all were."

Before I can say, "No clue," the slam of the front door alerts us to a new arrival.

"Hey, Mom, how are you?" A familiar male voice yells from the entryway.

I freeze in surprise, turning toward the door as if it would help me better process who walked into the house. I know that voice. What was Will doing here?

Will. Dr. Will Wunderliech. My high school friend and current ER coworker. He originally had my bracelet until he was shot by a minion and the *justitia* found its way into my scrub pocket. His mother was killed by a minion when he was a child and Smythe suspected Will's father met his death the same way.

How Will's parents came into possession of my *justitia* is a mystery. Smythe and I suspect they absconded with my *justitia* years ago, somehow stealing it from a magically locked vault in the Agency. Pure speculation. It makes sense, though, how else would it have fallen into their possession?

At any rate, Smythe determined Will's father was a mage, which makes Will a mage. He's not yet accepted his destiny. What's he doing here and why is he calling Mrs. Luckey "Mom?"

Smythe raises a brow as he gestures toward the door. He shares the same what-the-heck expression I'm sure my face mirrors. "I thought he said his mom died."

"She did."

"Is she," he gestures at the office doorway, "his foster mom?"

I shrug. "I don't know."

"I thought you guys were friends."

"It doesn't mean I hung out at his house and got cozy with his foster parents." But still. I should know the answer. Lesson learned? We don't always know our friends as well as we think.

Smythe grunts. "Pick a piece of paper to take with us. I'll tell you what I found when we get back to your place."

He taps a few more strokes on the keyboard as I grab a couple of sheets of paper, folding them in half for easier carrying. I'm halfway to the door, folded paper in hand, when Will pokes his head around the corner. Warmth floods my body. I offer him a grin while thrusting the folded paper behind my back. As soon as he recognizes me, his eyes widen then shrink into narrow slits.

"What are you two doing here?" His tone stings, a slap of accusation. "Mom said the FBI was looking through Dad's things."

I don't blame him for being mad. I'm pretty sure the last thing he wants is to run into me. No, make that the second to the last thing. The last being running into Smythe.

"We are investigating Richard Luckey's death."

Smythe steps around the desk to stand by me. "Are the Luckeys your foster parents?"

"They are." Will leans against the door jamb, arms crossed. "Again, why are you here? This was a suicide, not a demon invasion, or whatever it is you hunt."

I glance at Smythe, who stares at Will as if debating whether to tell him our suspicions. My mentor might disagree, but Will has a right to know what happened to his foster father.

"We think a demon influenced a large number of suicides over the last several days. From what we can tell, your father was the first one."

Smythe glares at me, a warning to keep silent. A little late to seal my lips. Not like I would've listened. Not on this matter.

"But Dad was a church deacon. How could a demon possess him?" Will's brows draw tight, yet a gleam in his eyes hints at his curiosity. "We didn't say he was possessed." I shake my head, negating the possibility, even though strong odds existed. I'd seen a demon possess a good person with dire results for the victim of the possession. "We're not sure what's going on. That's why we're here. Investigating."

"This is what you do? I thought you blew creatures to smithereens."

Smythe shifts like he has something to say. I place a hand on his arm, silent talk for *I've got this covered.* For once he obeys me, even if his jaw tenses hard enough to break teeth.

"Not quite. I mean, we do that too, but we also investigate. Have to make sure we know the reason behind the crimes and who's committing them before we make an arrest." I put finger quotes around "arrest."

Will's eyes narrow. "Is 'arrest' the new term for killing them?"

"Arrest sounds less violent." I shrug.

"And you really think Dad killed himself because of some demon?"

"Maybe," Smythe says, no longer able to obey my silent, I've-got-this-covered request. "We're here to determine if a demon was involved."

Will clamps his lips together as he looks at the floor. After a long pause, he raises his head, his eyes glinting with determination. "Okay. I'm in. You can train me as a mage. But only if I can help kill the bastard who did this."

Smythe blinks away surprise, a half-grin turning his lips. "Deal. I'll inform the Agency you want to be trained as a mage."

A good dose of shock wends through my veins. The last time we talked to Will, he refused to become a mage. Of course, he was grieving over the death of his wife, but still. He refused.

And to top it off, he's all but ignored me at work, keeping things professional instead of our usual cross into friendship. By professional, I mean chilly. As in, he only talks to me when necessary and then only if he can't find another nurse for the task.

Now he suddenly decides to embrace his birthright?

"So you'll do this for your foster dad, but not your parents?" I slap a hand over my mouth five seconds too late.

Good job, Gin. Only a worthless friend blurts out something so hurtful.

"I'm sorry. I shouldn't have said that."

Will covers the hurt with a go-to-hell glare. "His death is the proverbial straw on the camel's back. Everyone I loved has been killed by those damn demons. I need to do something about it."

I nod, too embarrassed to try to speak. Smythe answers for me.

"Good. We can always use another mage."

"I assume since you're here as the FBI, I'm not supposed to tell Mom any of this?"

"Correct. The less normals know, the better."

Normals? I've never heard Smythe use the term, but it fits. T doesn't count—he's about as normal as I was pre-*justitia*.

"What am I supposed to tell her?"

"Tell her the FBI was here—"

"No, I mean about being a mage. How long does the training take? I'd like to keep my job while training."

Smythe's jaw tightens while I bite the inside of my lip to keep from laughing. The Agency hates that I work at the ER, but at the same time, they refuse to pay me for being a *Justitian*. I have to live, so until they ante up, I'm continuing my job in the Emergency Department at Blue Forest. Nice to know Will feels the same. The Agency is going to love it.

Sarcasm is my middle name.

"Of course." Smythe might not like it, but clearly the man knows if his employer won't pay me—one of its demon-killing huntresses—the chances of it paying a new mage are slim. "I'll be in touch once we solve this case."

"Here's my number." Will rattles off his number to Smythe, who loads it into his phone's contact list.

"I'm glad you've had a change of heart." Smythe claps Will on the shoulder, a show of solidarity, while offering him his hand.

Clap, shake, and we're good to go.

Men.

My emotions ping around the room like a wayward pinball. Glad Will wants to be trained. Shocked Will wants to be trained. Mad Will treated me like an outcast for the last few months.

I'm about to get whiplash from emotional overload.

I pat Will on the shoulder too as I follow Smythe down the hall.

"Gin."

At my name, I stop, turn, give Will a raised brow.

"See you at work?" He mirrors my look, raised brow conveying a request for forgiveness.

I swallow away a snarky retort. "Sure. I'll be in tomorrow."

"Okay. See you then."

Flashing him a smile, I catch up to Smythe, who stands in the entryway, saying our thanks and good-byes to Mrs. Luckey.

A surge of happiness joins the wave of emotions pinging through me. Maybe everything will be okay between Will and me. Maybe our friendship will continue as it always had.

Hopefully, he feels the same.

Chapter Six

Smythe portals us back to my living room.

"What? No more demon hunting?" I drop the folded paper with Mr. Luckey's disturbing scrawl on the coffee table and rub my arms in an effort to erase the chill of traveling the in-between.

"We have several clues I want to upload."

"Like what? Besides the *Get away from me Satan* written on every piece of paper in his office?" I shove the papers toward Smythe who sits on the couch waiting for his laptop to power up.

He glances at them, a small shudder running through his limbs. "That is creepy. But, I was referring to his brokerage accounts."

Brokerage accounts? "What do brokerage accounts have to do with demon hunting? And how do you know he had some?"

Smythe raises a brow. Oh, right. He's an ace hacker. Which explains what he was doing on Mr. Luckey's computer.

"As I was saying, he lost a bunch of money. Not enough to wipe them out, but enough to upset anyone of retirement age. I wouldn't think it would be enough to cause someone to want to kill themselves."

"But maybe it was enough to upset him and the demon saw an opening and struck."

"You mentioned earlier about a dream man."

Icy blood wends through my veins as the memory replays. A cold bead of sweat tickles my spine. I cross my arms, trying to appear nonchalant.

"Yeah? What about him?"

"Why was he visiting you?"

"How the hell am I supposed to know?" More like no way in hell am I going to tell you. "He visited. End of story."

"Were you going to take his offer?"

Heat slaps my cheeks while my stomach shakes as if my innards were dipped in ice. Should I tell him? I rub cold hands against my arms.

"I wanted to." My voice drops to a whisper. "I wanted to really badly."

A muscle by his eye twitches. "Do you think the same thing happened to Richard Luckey?"

"How should I know?" I shrug. "Maybe. Maybe not. I'm not even sure what talked to me was real."

"I felt it in your head. Earlier. It's real."

Shivers course through me and I wrap my arms around my waist in a vain effort to hold them inside.

"Thanks. That makes me feel so much better."

"Think, Gin. Does your *justitia* know?"

"It won't say. I asked."

"Try again. Maybe it knows. While you attempt to talk to it, I'll look up despair demons. See if one of them has the ability to project itself into a human's mind."

"Okay. But first I'm going to get some warm tea. The portal was cold." Little white lies never hurt anyone. And it wasn't a total lie—the portal really was cold. But the chills wracking my body have little to do with the portal and a lot to do with the dream man. Who wouldn't get the shivers imagining something invading their mind?

While Smythe types away, I make myself a cup of hot tea. Once the microwave dings, I grab the cup and sit at the table, wondering if my *justitia* wanted to chat. Judging by its lack of reaction, it doesn't.

Three sips later and I close my eyes, delving deep into my mind, until the pulsing, purple energy of the *justitia* appears shimmering around my nerves.

I close my eyes, focusing on the *justitia's* energy, hoping it deigns to answer me.

Was it a demon in my mind talking to me? Asking me to come to him?

After a long pause, silver links shift around my wrist. Energy flares along my nerves. The eerie voice of the *justitia* echoes in my mind.

Demon not have body.

Relief rushes through my system. Yes! My *justitia* is going to give me insight into what demonic entity caused all these suicides.

Is that a yes?

Demon not have body.

Okay. "Yes" might be a simple word, but apparently my *justitia* can't say it.

I rub the bridge of my nose, trying to think like a *justitia*, a single-minded focus on killing demons coupled with an amazing ability to avoid answering questions. My forehead aches with the effort.

If the demon doesn't have a body, then how did he get into my mind? Provided he actually got in there. Maybe Smythe and T read the situation wrong.

Powerful demon.

If he was so powerful, why didn't you form a

sword? Why did you stay in bracelet form?

Demon not have body.

I draw in a deep breath through my nose. Hold it for a count of ten. *So, you only turn into a sword in the physical presence of a demon? A virtual demon doesn't count?*

Only change for demon. No demon. No sword.

And because this demon appears in my mind, then you stay as a bracelet?

Only change for demon. No demon. No sword.

But the demon was in my mind? Right?

Demon not have body.

I purse my lips together, unable to throttle the thing. *You keep saying that.*

Listen.

I am! I want to know if it was really a demon and if so, which one?

Powerful demon.

Is that all you can say about him? No name? Nothing else?

I get the impression the thing huffs. Surely it's not as aggravated at me as I am at it?

Demon offers. Uses mind. Human dies. Demon feeds.

You're telling me the demon feeds off dying humans?

Feeds off sad humans. Sad humans die. Demon happy.

Good thing telepathy doesn't require me to open my tense jaw to speak. *Then why didn't you say something when the demon appeared to me? I almost took him up on his offer.*

The *justitia* pauses. *Demon not have body.*

I know that! He was in my mind. But why didn't you say something?

You sad. No listen.

Now it's my turn to pause, mulling over its words. No listen? *You mean, you tried to talk to me and I wouldn't listen?*

You no listen.

But you tried?

Yes. You block. No listen.

Being hungover prohibits the *justitia* from talking to me? What a stupid thing to do.

I'm sorry.

The bracelet shakes, acknowledgement and forgiveness rolled into one. At least someone currently in this house forgives me.

Unlike Smythe, who won't even listen to my explanation. Something I need to rectify. As soon as I finish talking with my *justitia*.

I promise to listen to you from now on.

Another rattle of the silver links. Another acceptance of my words.

How do you kill this demon?

Sword.

Duh. I mean, where do we find him? How close does he have to be to project himself into a victim's mind? How does he choose his victims?

Human sad. Demon feed.

He can feed from wherever he is? Or does he have to appear physically?

Close. Not touch human to feed.

So how do we catch him?

No catch demon. Demon catch you.

Wonderful. Just what I needed to hear.

Since my *justitia* seems to be in a sharing mood, I continue with other questions. The ones I've wanted an answer to for some time.

What happened to you after the last Justitian *who wore you died? I know you were locked in a safe at the Agency, but how did you escape? How did you get from Will's possession to my scrub pocket?*

It waits long enough for me to think it refuses to answer. Again. Right when I'm about to give up, its eerie voice drifts into my mind, soft and scared.

Dark vault.

Whoo-hoo! It decided to answer. *Then what happened?*

Light. Voices. No Justitian. Mages. Other.

Other? What do you mean, other?

Other. No mage. No demon. No human. Other.

Makes perfect sense. I pinch the bridge of my nose. Can't complain, though. I'm the one who wanted answers.

As an exercise in frustration, I continue my line of questioning.

How did you get from Will's possession into my scrub pocket?

I get the distinct impression the thing chuckles.

Wish.

Yours or his?

Both. Sense Justitian. Want away from minion. Not safe.

Wasn't that the understatement of the year?

He wanted you safe, so he put you in my pocket without me realizing what he'd done?

Another chuckle. *Me wish. He wish. Me obey. You wear. All good.*

64

I suppose Will slipped the *justitia* into my scrub pocket without me realizing it. Which wouldn't have been hard to do since I was a little distracted watching him bleed out from where a minion shot him. Although I'd swear he never touched my pocket, never slipped the silver-linked bracelet inside.

Why were you taken out of the vault?

It speaks after a long pause. *Why no.*

You mean you don't know why?

Yes. Why no.

Apparently, I wasn't the only one clueless to the goings on at the Agency.

Thank you for talking with me.

Me like you.

I like you too. Warmth spreads through my limbs as if the entity in my bracelet gives me a full-body hug.

It likes me. After all that's happened the last few days, its words make the heavy weight on my chest lessen. Drawing in a deep breath, I open my eyes.

My tea sits cold on the table in front of me. How long had I been carrying on a conversation? The clock on the wall states thirty minutes. Huh. I could have sworn we only talked for a couple of minutes. I wonder what Smythe found on his computer.

After putting the mug on the counter, I walk into the living room. Smythe sits in his usual position, feet propped on the coffee table, laptop up and running on his thighs. Unlike usual, his fingers rest against his legs.

"You find something?"

At my words, he startles, turning to me, eyebrows raised. "Yeah, you?"

What was he thinking while staring at the screen? Pondering the case? Wondering about our relationship?

Dreaming of ways to apologize to me?

I wish. Swallowing the urge to pick an argument, I offer him a quick half-grin. I'll ask him later. After we solve this case.

"Yeah. You first."

"According to the Agency records, there have been a couple of instances of despair demons causing despair instead of feeding off what was already there."

"No surprise. They are despair demons, after all. I'd think they'd cause it as well as be attracted to it. Was there any mention of a demon invading minds? Or dreams? And influencing a person while inside their head?"

He shakes his head. "Not any I found. The Agency hasn't digitalized all its scrolls though, so it's possible there's more about it in the Agency library. What did you find out?"

I know something Smythe doesn't. For once. A grin creeps across my lips. "My *justitia* said a powerful demon could invade the minds of sad people and feed off them when they die. The man in what I thought a dream was really a demon."

Smythe's eyes widen for a second. "So you have been haunted by a despair demon. That might help us find him."

"Always good to be of service." My grin turns brittle. Who wants a despair demon haunting them? Definitely not me. Especially since the thing is in my mind and not appearing physically where I can off its ass.

"Did you learn anything else?"

I shrug. "Yeah. I asked how it got in my scrub pocket and it said it wished to be with the *Justitian*. I'm a little shaky on the how. I mean, Will had to have put it in my pocket, right?

"The *justitia* might have wished to be with me, but it couldn't just poof and appear so Will must've slipped it into my pocket without realizing it." Yep, that sounded ridiculous to my ears and I'm the one speaking.

"Interesting. It doesn't explain how it got out of the vault."

"Nope. Just said others helped it. As in not a mage, not a human, not a demon. An 'other.'"

Smythe cocks a brow. "An other?"

"No clue. It wouldn't say." I offer him a half-shrug and get back to the more pressing topics of a demon invading peoples' minds and my growling stomach. "So are we interviewing any other families? Are you hungry? It's lunchtime."

Smythe looks at the time on his laptop. "So it is. Why don't we grab something, then talk to the most recent victim's family?"

"You think they wrote *Get away from me Satan* on every piece of paper they could find?"

"Probably not. But you never know. We need to check it out. Come on." He closes his laptop and stands.

Chapter Seven

Lunch turns out to be a win, an all-you-can-eat buffet at a Mediterranean restaurant. A perfect place to stuff yourself with food while mostly ignoring your tablemate. No sense in causing a scene in public that gets me labeled "crazy woman with a grudge." Thank you, too much food, for keeping my mouth shut. The restaurant makes up for trying to meet with the family of the last victim, Trisha Fluke. When we get to her house, no one is home. A quick Internet check on my phone shows the funeral starts in an hour.

"Let's go to the funeral home."

Opening my car door, I give Smythe a raised-brow glare. "Seriously? You really expect the husband to talk to us at his wife's funeral?"

After a two second pause, during which time he peers at me over the roof of my car as if I'm the odd one, he nods once. "Yes, I do."

"Why?" I raise a brow. "Going to use the compulsion spell? That's not nice on a good day."

He shrugs. "It's effective. We could wait until tomorrow, but if we hurry, we can get there before the funeral starts and talk with the husband."

I shake my head at his audacity, yet slide into the car and start the engine. Yeah, it's crass to accost a grieving family member at their loved one's funeral, but at the same time, Smythe has a point. Waiting even another day will allow the demon to strike more victims, to take more lives. The quicker we can solve this mystery, the quicker we can take another demon off the streets.

Provided I can kill this one.

I'm no longer confident in my abilities.

What if the demon invades my mind again? What if this time it convinces me to follow him? Worse, what if the only way to stop him is to do what he wants? What would happen to me then? Maybe letting him give me eternal rest wasn't as bad as it sounded.

Oh, hell, who am I fooling? Of course it's as bad as it sounded. One, I'd be dead. Two, I'm not convinced the demon wouldn't haul my ass to Hell. On the other hand, it would eliminate the guilt I feel about Donny.

Assuming one doesn't feel guilt in the afterlife.

"Gin?" At the sound of my name on Smythe's tongue, I snap back to reality. "You gonna drive or sit there?"

"Right. Sorry." *Way to look smart, Gin.* I shift the car into drive. "Just getting the path to the funeral home in my mind."

"Really?" I don't need to take my eyes off the road to know he shoots me a what-the-hell glare. "Because the route is on my GPS."

Busted. I clear my throat. "It could be in my mind."

"Uh-huh." He shakes his head. "Turn left here at the light."

I do as he says, following his directions until we reach the funeral home. A parking lot full of cars greets us. As soon as I step out of my car, I stop, turning to Smythe.

"I can't go in there. I'm not dressed for a funeral."

I'm in tan slacks and heels and look damn professional, but a funeral in Dallas was a completely different thing. Black clothing was the only way to go. Smythe isn't any better, dressed in jeans and long-sleeved navy T-shirt combo. "You aren't dressed for it either. Maybe we should try again tomorrow."

He stares at me long enough for me to wonder if I sprouted a third eye. "What?"

"Oh, ye of little faith." Whispered words roll off his tongue, a spell of shimmering light surrounding me.

Like a transparent bubble, light shimmers around my body. But I'm still in my tan slacks and heels. I glance at Smythe, noting the shimmering light surrounding him, a pale gleam easily missed if you weren't observant, and do a double take. Instead of jeans and a navy tee, he's in a dark suit complete with a tie, black dress shoes replacing his shitkickers.

What the heck?

"You changed." Nothing like pointing out the obvious in a holy-heck situation.

"You did too." He gestures at me.

"Into what?"

"Black dress and heels. Like you wore to Blake's funeral."

I stiffen at the memory of Blake's death. Losing Blake left a hole in my heart, a hole slowly being filled in by Smythe.

Until he misread the scene with Donny and thought the football star and I had something going on.

As if I could leave Smythe for some gigolo. Clearly my mentor had issues. And I had an oversized ache in my chest coupled with guilt and depression.

No wonder the despair demon haunted my dreams.

I probably tasted like ambrosia.

"Thanks." I swallow, shoving all thoughts of Blake to the black shadows in my mind. "What's the game plan?"

"I'll do the talking. Don't worry. He won't remember us."

"Seriously? You can wipe his mind?"

"The power of suggestion."

Like Smythe's father, David, the Agency's Head Mage-In-Charge, did with me after minions attacked the Agency. He wiped several minutes of my mind clean trying to get me to admit how I managed to blast the attackers. Luckily, I didn't spill my secret of Zagan giving me his demonic power. Something tells me the knowledge wouldn't go over so well with David.

Smythe is already several steps ahead of me, clearly under the impression I'm right behind him instead of lost in my thoughts. I lengthen my stride, catching him as he opens the door to the funeral home.

A crowd of people stands inside, milling around, speaking in hushed voices. Smythe looks both ways before walking down the hall to the left. To the right are a set of double doors opening into the chapel, rows of pews filled with friends and family of the deceased. I give the chapel a quick glance before following Smythe.

We pass the restrooms and the offices before arriving at the family mourning room. Smythe walks in like he knew the deceased woman. Which causes all attention to land on us.

All the better to work the spell.

Smythe holds up his hand, mutters words I don't catch, and all eyes glaze over except for one. A dark-haired, medium height, overweight man in his thirties focuses his gaze on us. I assume it's Trisha's husband, Chris (I know his name from the Internet search of her funeral) since he's our person of interest. His eyes widen with shock or surprise. Smythe walks toward him while talking.

"We need to ask you some questions. What happened the night your wife died?"

"Who are—"

Smythe gives a sharp command in a language not related to English and Chris stands still, mouth agape, face slack. Second spell accomplished.

"What happened the night your wife died?"

"We watched TV." The monotone quality of the man's voice is almost hypnotic. "She was upset because she'd gotten laid off. For whatever reason, she thought it was her fault upper management were dicks. She looks at me, says she loves me, then she leaves the room.

"I thought she was going to bed, but when I went to bed, she was underwater in the bathtub. An empty wine bottle was on the floor along with medicine bottles. She'd taken the rest of my epilepsy medicine as well as the rest of our pain pills. I called the ambulance, but it was too late." He sniffs, tears streaming down his face.

"I'm sorry for your loss." Smythe grabs a tissue from the box on a conveniently located table and hands it to Chris. "Was she suicidal?"

Chris sniffs, wiping his eyes and nose with the tissue. "Never been depressed a day in her life. Always happy. I mean, she got sad on occasion, but nothing long-lasting. Her getting laid off was a bump in the road, you know? She would've gotten another job and we would've been fine. Why did she have to kill herself?" His words end on a sob.

Smythe pats him on the shoulder. "Did she talk about Satan or the Devil?"

"Like how?"

"Did she think they were trying to talk to her?"

Chris's dark brows furrow over disbelieving eyes. "You think she was crazy?"

"Didn't say that. I want to know if she thought someone was talking to her."

"Not that I know of. She wasn't nuts."

Smythe gives Chris another pat on the shoulder, whispers words next to the grieving man's cheek. Chris visibly relaxes, his shoulders dropping away from his ears.

"Forget you saw us. Forget you talked to us. And if someone tries to talk to you in your dreams, ignore him."

After one last pat on the shoulder, Smythe steps away from the man. We step out of the room before Smythe waves his hand, releasing the family from his compulsion spell. Sorrow hangs in the air, a fog of melancholy and grief. We walk out of the funeral home, ignoring as best as possible the mourning friends and family. When we get into the car and shut the doors, I turn to Smythe.

"What did you tell him there at the end? To make him relax?"

He raises a brow. "I told him everything would be okay and pushed the thought into him."

"But what if it's not okay? His wife died."

Some things never become okay. Livable, yes.

Okay, no. And the number one item on the Things-Never-To-Tell-A-Grieving-Person list is "Everything will be okay." Smythe should know that. It's not like it's a secret.

He shakes his head at my tone, a silent negation of my words.

"Eventually, if you stick around long enough, things even out. Become okay. It wasn't a lie. And it helped him relax."

Memories dart out of hiding as anger and heat run roughshod through my veins. "Bullshit." I slap a hand against the steering wheel. "Things don't always magically become okay. Sometimes they remain sucky and you learn to hide all the ugly behind a wall of glam and glitter. The underneath is still nasty and eats away at you."

"What are you referring to?" Smythe shoots me brow-furrowed surprise. "Bad things happen to everyone. It's how you deal with them that matters. If you don't hold on to them, they smooth out."

"Really?" I gesture between the two of us. "So we're all smoothed out now? Because somehow I doubt it." My glare obliterates the little voice in my mind telling me to shut the hell up. "You left me to defend myself against a demon!"

"Are you sure? Don't you think I would've known if there was a demon in the club?"

"Obviously you didn't! You clearly walked right by it since you were storming off in a huff of self-righteousness. And you wouldn't—won't—let me explain."

"You led me on and then you kissed Donny!" Anger in his voice rattles the windows.

On any other day, I'd back down, maybe even act scared. But I'm pumped on my own anger, my own sense of betrayal. He can't scare me.

"You won't let me explain! I did not kiss him! He kissed me. There's a difference. You walked in a split-second before I was about to kick him in the 'nads. Then you walked out without listening. I could have died and you were too busy planning your pity-party to notice!"

His jaw tenses. "I don't want to do this right now."

"What do you mean, not right now? If not now then when? We need to work this out."

"Not now, Gin."

"Why not?"

"Not now!" Giving me a glare, he holds his hand up, mutters his portal forming words and ends our conversation by disappearing from the car.

Damn it, damn it, damn it.

Since when did he learn to form an overhead portal? Who cares when or how he perfected his portal forming ability, the point being he poofed himself out of a conversation before I was finished yelling at him.

Damn mage.

Anger makes another trip across my already irritated system, leaving behind a pounding headache, a churning stomach and a thundering heart. I use deep breathing techniques to try and calm my racing pulse, which does nothing to ease the urge to slap the shit out of my mentor. If anything, it makes it worse.

So much for channeling my inner yogi.

After hitting the steering wheel a couple more times—smarting my palms, yet doing nothing for the Smythe problem—I throw the car into gear and head home. My thoughts whirl between our fight, how aggravating men are, and the demon causing all these suicides.

Can I stop the demon? I can't even convince my mentor I didn't betray him. Nor could I kill the last demon I fought. What were the chances of killing this one? What if this one defeated me too?

Was I really qualified to being a demon huntress?

Silver links rattle against my wrist, a reminder I wear a *justitia*, and therefore I'm supposed to be awesome.

I'm not. I'm a relapsed alcoholic with an empath problem and a prickly mage as my guardian and wanna-be lover. After today it's doubtful we'll ever get back together.

And that bothers me more than the rampaging demon of despair.

Some demon huntress I am.

Chapter Eight

As soon as I pull into the drive, T pulls in behind me. I park in the garage and wait until he catches up to me before shutting the garage door.

"You okay?" He greets me with a hug coupled with a quizzical look.

"Yeah, sure, why?"

"Your make-up is running down your face."

I swipe my hands under my eyes, fingers coming away with black streaks. Lovely. "Smythe and I got into a fight while at the last victim's funeral. Guess I got more upset than I thought." And I thought I was pretty damn upset. Shows you what I know.

T wraps an arm around my shoulders. "I hope you gave him hell."

"I guess. He portaled out of the car after telling me he didn't want to discuss it."

T cracks a grin, gives my shoulder a couple of pats. "It's a start. Come on, let's go inside and figure out dinner."

He leads the way, pushing open the door from the garage to the back porch, then unlocking the kitchen door. I walk straight into the living room, leaving my twin in the kitchen to grab a cold beer.

I look at the coffee table, part of me hoping to see Smythe's laptop. No such luck. Both the laptop and black backpack are gone, evidence my mentor portaled into my locked house and took his things.

This time all I feel is crushing sadness. He's gone. What if he doesn't return?

I really need to get a handle on my spiraling emotions. But knowing and doing are two separate things.

Drawing in a deep breath, I flip on the TV. Scenes from Donny's funeral dance across the screen. I change channels, only to see another shot from a different angle.

"What's on?" T says.

I jump, drop the remote onto the empty coffee table and slap a hand over my chest, as if the motion would calm my racing heart.

"Geez, T, you scared the crap out of me."

"Sorry." He grabs the remote, switching it to a cable news show. "Not the best, but better than what was on. Now, what do you want for dinner? I'll cook."

"You've cooked the last several nights. It's my turn."

"Whatever. I'm good."

"I'll help."

He shrugs. "Why don't you go clean up and I'll pull out steaks?"

"Okay." I shut the door to my bedroom behind me before heading to my bathroom. A quick glance in the mirror makes me suck in a breath. Mascara streaks down my cheeks, giving me the appearance of a creature from a horror movie.

I grab a washcloth and wipe off the streaks along with the rest of my makeup. At least my dull brown hair remains in its twist.

After I finish in the bathroom, I change out of my

professional clothes into a baggy T-shirt and lounge-around-the-house pants. Ahhh. Nothing beats the feeling of comfy clothes at the end of a long day. Dinner, here I come.

I pull open my bedroom door, my shoulders back, boobs thrust forward like a model showing her wares. A niggling thought that I've done this before pings my mind, a sense of unease.

My *justitia* fires into a sword the moment I step into the hall. Was Zagan here? At a sharp intake of breath from the kitchen, I realize it wasn't Zagan. First, my *justitia* always reacted with a happy dance to the demon of deceit, not a sword. Even when it was already in sword form, it couldn't strike a killing blow to Zagan, its maker, its friend.

Which meant a demon or minion was in my house.

With T.

Shit.

I dart into the kitchen and come to a stop. Rahab, the demon of pride, the demon I fought and lost to the night I killed Donny, stands in the middle of my kitchen, holding a knife to T's throat. T's hands grip Rahab's arm, keeping the knife from pricking his skin. Fear and anger light T's eyes.

Memories play in my mind, in my twin's mind, the same memories of our father threatening T to make me do degrading things. A shudder crawls down my spine. Our bastard of a father deserved to die. And unlike how I felt about killing Donny, with my father I didn't feel a hint of grief, only fear of being caught.

But T and I were grown now, not teenagers, not children hiding in fear. We were adults. And one of us had a demon-killing sword.

Killing a demon the second time is a charm.

Hopefully.

"Gin, how nice to see you again." Rahab's voice curls against my skin.

"What are you doing in my house?" I raise my *justitia* diagonally in front of my chest, a warning of what is to come.

His gaze bounces from my face to the sword and back. Thin lips tighten, relax, as if he's not impressed with my show of arms.

Why would he be? The last time he fought me he won.

"Paying a visit. You took something of mine so turnabout is fair play. And what a nice gift it is too." He tilts his head toward my twin.

T's eyes narrow as he tugs on the demon's arm to no avail. If anything, the knife draws closer to his throat. A dark aura surrounds T, air warping from his anger deep inside threatening to explode.

My "gifts" consist of empathic ability coupled with a touch-and-see problem, but talking with ghosts isn't the only trick in T's repertoire.

If only his powers had manifested when we were children instead of in our late teens, our father wouldn't have made our lives a living hell.

The fridge starts to vibrate, a low rumble rattling the beer bottles in the door, the clinking a nerve-grating noise. If the demon knew what was good for him, he'd release T now.

Since when are demons smart?

Rahab's gaze flicks to the fridge, back to me. "Your appliance is not working correctly. A matter you'll no longer need to deal with after I'm done with you. Revenge is mine."

He tries to shove the knife into T's throat, but I'm running the few steps between us, my *justitia* slicing through his arm, missing T's fingers by millimeters. T ducks and turns, fist raised as if to nail the demon in the crotch, while I pull the sword back for another try, but Rahab disappears, leaving my sword singing through the air.

"Are you—" Before I can get out "okay" I'm grabbed by the hair, tossed into the wall face-first with a bone-cracking thud. My *justitia* shuts down the pain turning my nose into a throbbing ball of fire.

Damn it. How many times could I break my snout?

Shaking off the pain, I turn around right in time to see Rahab pitch T against the wall above the table. My twin bounces, landing on the table with a groan. Red dots my vision. This demon was going down.

I rush toward Rahab, only to be thrown across the room by a demonic energy burst. I land with a thud on top of T, who releases an 'oomph' on an expulsion of air. His eyes widen.

You okay?

He nods. *Go kill the fucker.*

On my way. Shoving myself off my twin, I slide to the floor, sword pointed at a shit-grinning Rahab.

"You are a slow learner, eh?" He takes a step toward me.

Ignoring his comment, I rush him, only to be thrown telekinetically into the doorframe leading to the living room, like some sort of sick game of pitch with me as the ball. Effing demons and their telekinetic powers.

Before I can get up, Rahab is on top of me, his

heavy weight pushing my body against the cool linoleum floor. Large hands encircle my throat, squeezing. Black spots dart across my vision as I aim my sword at his neck.

Or try to.

My arm twitches on the ground. It takes my oxygen deprived brain a couple of seconds to realize my arm won't move because his knee jams into my biceps. I struggle, trying to dislodge him, trying to get my sword in a position to slash at his leg, when a rumble shakes the floor.

I might not be able to move my head, but I know evidence of T's anger when it rolls around a room. Lights flicker. Rahab eases his grip on my neck enough for me to draw in a deep breath of much needed air. He shifts, turning his attention from me to my twin, shifts enough for me to wiggle my arm out from under his knee.

I draw my arm back, ready to slice into his side, when he notices my movement. Too fast to track, he raises my head, slamming it onto the hard floor. Lights flicker, but I'm no longer sure if it's due to T's anger or a concussion.

Relax. Come to me. The despair demon's voice floats through my mind, followed by a compulsion hard to resist. I want to come to him, to do what he wants, to lose this fight. Peace beckons, a promise only he gives.

But if I give in, T dies. While I can throw away my life, giving in to the hidden depression consuming me, knowingly ending my twin's is a whole other matter.

My *justitia* tremors, snapping me out of the spell. Seriously? Was I actually considering listening to one demon while fighting another? Have I lost my mind?

Yeah, not going there. I'm afraid of the answer.

Fuck off, demon. I snap barriers around my mind. Or try to. Kind of hard to pull off while lying on my back with a throbbing head and possible concussion. Since the despair demon offers no further requests, I assume I'm successful.

Of course, we all know what happens when you assume.

The floor shakes, surprise loosens Rahab's grip on me. Drawing in a deep breath, I blink away the spots edging my vision as he rises onto his knees, hands held toward T.

"What kind of freak are you?"

"One who won't let you kill my sister." Voice pitched in a low rumble, T takes a step forward, hands held out to his sides, palms facing us.

The next second T drops to his knees, fear erasing the confidence in his wide eyes.

"Humans. You forget with whom you are dealing."

A flash of energy explodes from Rahab's hands, flinging my twin against the wall with a bone crunching snap. T slumps to the ground, eyes closed, the shaking floor stilling.

I scream, twist, and manage to slice my sword into the demon's leg. Rahab lets loose with a screech. He draws back his fist, but I slam my *justitia* into his side. With another screech, he rolls off me, clutching his bleeding injury, black blood seeping between his fingers. I scramble out of the way, scooting across the linoleum on my butt while pointing my sword at the irate demon.

The counter presses against my back, stops my movement, but gives me enough support to try standing upright. Two Rahabs stand before me snarling.

"Bitch."

"Bastard."

Blinking in a vain attempt to eradicate one of the demons, I focus on keeping the sword pointed at Rahab. The problem being which Rahab to point it at.

Iridescent lights sparkle behind him in my living room for a second before Smythe and a bunch of other mages step out of a portal. Or maybe it's just Smythe. I squint. Nope, judging by the different clothing colors, it's not just Smythe come to save me. I shake my head and the twin forms merge together. Ah-ha. Smythe brought three mages.

To kill one demon.

No wonder I'm losing.

Since I'm staring over his shoulder with a slight grin on my lips, Rahab jerks his head around, his eyes widening at the mages.

Way to give away their game, Gin. Although what could I expect with a concussion? Thinking straight is not a part of my current abilities.

"Fuck." The demon takes a step away from the line of mages, proving his intelligence. At least in knowing when to run from the good guys.

Energy balls thrown by the arriving mages slam into the wall, missing Rahab, but exploding drywall into stinging pellets. Before I can move, he gives me a quick shit-eating grin. With a flick of his fingers, my body shoots up to the ceiling, slamming into the plaster hard enough to crack it. And then I'm dropping, gravity yanking me down, down, down as if I've been thrown from a much greater height. Crushing pain registers for a half second as my back slams against the floor, as breath explodes from injured lungs, as the cracking of bones ricochets around the room.

Oh, sh—

But darkness pulls me under before I can finish the thought.

Chapter Nine

I wake to softness under my back. Softness? Where am I? An effort to open my eyes proves futile, as if boulders sit on my lids. Okay, then. Breathing, deep and rhythmic, drifts into my ear.

Recent memories rush into my mind, banishing some of my confusion. A demon fight with me as the loser. Which means I should be lying on my kitchen floor instead of whatever softness cushions me. Unless I dreamed the whole demon fight. Maybe I'm asleep. Maybe it's Smythe lying beside me in bed. Maybe I didn't really kill Donny and we're still together.

Somehow, I doubt it.

Which means I truly fought Rahab and lost. Again. So where am I?

The breathing hitches, a slight movement jostles me, followed by shuffling noises, like someone turning over in bed. I am in a bed.

One problem solved. Who was beside me?

Another deep inhale, this time to my right. Multiple people? In my room? At least I'm assuming it's my room. I might have solved the original question of what surface lies beneath me, but clearly opened a whole other list of who, what, and how queries.

If only I could pry my eyelids open, I could answer a good deal of those questions.

No such luck. Maybe twitch a finger? Putting all

my energy into moving my pointer finger, I tell my body to move. To no avail.

Panic shoots through my system, punching into my solar plexus with a one-two blow. I gasp, the motion popping open my lids. Trembling shakes my limbs, rattles my teeth. Cold. So very cold.

The ceiling stares down at me, little bumps in its textured surface seeming to laugh, to tease.

"Gin?" T's voice is followed by a touch on my left arm.

"Gin?" A touch on my right follows Smythe's voice.

I blink at the bluish-hued laughing ceiling. Ceilings don't laugh, right? Right. No laughing ceilings. Except for mine. I want to ask why they don't notice whatever is up there, but my teeth rattle in their sockets, my limbs tremoring like I'm seizing.

"Eloise!" T yells, but instead of reverberating in my ear, it sounds like he's in a tunnel. Or maybe I'm in the tunnel. Maybe there's a bed with a laughing ceiling in a concrete tunnel.

Maybe I'm tripping.

The ceiling continues its maniacal laughter, its bluish hue drawing closer until I no longer see anything except a sea of deep blue.

Sea of blue…sea of blue…sea of blue…

Healing. I'm being healed by the Agency's albino healer, Eloise.

My lids drift shut.

The next time my eyes open when I gasp for air. My gaze fixates on the white, non-laughing ceiling. Right. Because ceilings don't laugh, have grins, nor do they stare at a person. Unless the person has issues.

I am not going there.

T sits to my left on the bed. Smythe kneels on the floor to my right, holding my hand in his large palm. A slight rustle of clothing sounds from behind my head. Eloise. Her presence fills my bedroom as if the air sings in her proximity. I tilt my head back, stare into her sightless red eyes as she stands over me at the foot of my bed. I lay upside down on the bed, feet propped on my pillow, my typical healing position.

When I open my lips to speak, I have to swallow several times before the words will come out, my tongue thick and dry against the roof of my mouth.

"Thank you." I say those words to her so often it's like a cracked record hopping in the same spot over and over and over.

She nods, lips turning in a gentle smile.

"What happened?" Yeah, I remember the demon fight, the way Rahab played toss Gin into the walls and ceiling, the pain of landing crumpled and broken on the kitchen floor. But everything afterward remains a dark well of missing information.

"You were hurt." Smythe squeezes my hand before releasing it like I have the plague. His gaze skitters off my face faster than a roach darts out of the light.

I wish he'd listen and believe me when I tell him nothing happened. He should know me better, but emotional pain prohibits reasoning and it's clear from the way he prefers to look at the ground his pain hurts as deep as mine.

Which doesn't excuse his behavior.

"Eloise came after the demon escaped." T interrupts my thoughts, snapping me back to the question I asked and promptly forgot about once

Smythe spoke. What happened after lights out, sucka. "You've been out for a day."

A day? A whole day? Wait, that makes it Wednesday. I'm supposed to be in the ER today. Oh shit.

"What?" This time my words have no problem crossing a thick and dry tongue. "Did I miss work?"

Say no, please, say no.

T, Smythe and Eloise exchange a look, somewhere between wondering if the healing didn't completely work and needing to lie. Crap, I could lose my job if I missed a day without calling in. After the last time, my boss Ruth, a.k.a Nurse Hatchet, wouldn't be so generous to let me off with only a write-up.

"Oh god, I'm gonna be fired." My eyes close, my shaky hands resting on top of them as if the motion will make the day restart. My stomach makes a pit and drops my heart into it.

What will I do without my job? How will I pay the bills?

"I called in for you."

My hands drop as I stare through blurry eyes at a serious T. I bet that went over well with Ruth, the stickler for speaking with the ill employee.

"How—"

"Told her you were bad sick. She wanted a doctor's note." He shrugs, a grin tugging at the corners of his lips. "Guess she didn't believe me."

"Thanks, but I'm still screwed sideways."

"I wrote you a note," Eloise says.

My eyes widen as my breath hitches in shocked lungs. "You have official doctor's office letterhead? Because she won't accept anything less. I'm surprised she even took your call, T. She doesn't normally speak to anyone except the employee who's ill."

Eloise touches my shoulder, her gaze zeroing in on mine. "The paper and note will look official, don't worry."

Air rushes out of my lungs on a whoosh of relief. "Thank you. I seem to say those words a lot to you."

"That's what friends are for." She taps my shoulder twice. "Now, be sure to rest, you had a nasty blow to the head. You're lucky I was available."

Translation: you would've died without my healing.

I swing my legs over the side of the bed—causing Smythe to take a step back—and pause until a swirl of dizziness stops making the room spin. Then I launch myself at Eloise, wrapping my arms around her waist, hugging her for all I am worth.

She saved my life so many times I've lost count.

"I'm glad you're my friend."

She pats my back before pulling away.

"So Gin's okay?" Smythe asks. "No lingering effects?"

"None," Eloise replies. "She had a hard blow and still needs rest but she's fine."

"Good." My mentor nods. "I need to check on some things at the Agency. I'll be back tomorrow."

"How did you know to come?"

He raises a brow. "The demon notification program alerted us to Rahab's presence."

"It worked?" And in my favor too? What were the chances?

His stare lasts a beat too long. Heat flushes my cheeks. *Good observation, Gin.* Of course it worked.

They came and chased off the demon before he caused me irreparable damage.

"Thanks for coming." I want to reach for him, to offer an apology without words, but clasp my hands together before they can move. No matter the gratitude rushing through me, he needs to be the one apologizing to me.

But oh, how I want to touch him.

After a lingering stare followed by another nod, he mutters words sounding suspiciously like Latin, steps into his portal and disappears. A puff of warm air from the portal swirls around my ankles. At least he stuck around to find out whether or not I'd be okay.

It might have been simply to ensure his mentee lived, but I prefer to think it was because he actually cared about me, maybe even realized he was wrong about Donny and me. And since it's just me and my thoughts, I can believe whatever I want.

Sometimes delusions are all one has.

"Ass," T's voice snaps me out of my thoughts. "You'd think he'd stick around longer."

"Sometimes giving one's all seems like so little to others." Eloise stares at where Smythe disappeared.

I step around her, throwing my arms around my twin and squeezing until he pats my back.

"I thought you were hurt bad."

"I thought you were dead."

Peace flows through both of us, the other's touch a calming balm for our souls. What would I have done if Rahab had killed my twin? What would T have done if I'd died?

Thoughts to shove to the back of my mind to review on another day.

A squeak of springs indicates Eloise sits on my bed. Sits. As if she plans on staying.

T releases me to plop down next to her. He smiles at her. She grins at him. Great. The lovebirds are in my bedroom. T cuts me a glare like he heard my thoughts.

I did hear your thoughts.

Great.

I crawl onto the middle the bed so I can look at both of them while talking. "What happened after I blacked out? You mentioned Rahab escaped?"

Eloise nods while T answers.

"I blacked out too, but woke in time to see him hop a portal right after he slammed you into the ground." His jaw tenses. "I hope to never see you hurt again. Damn demon. You really need to quit this job."

"We've been over this." Now it's my turn for the clenched jaw.

Eloise's head turns from T to me as if she's never heard siblings argue.

"T," Eloise pats my twin's thigh, her voice a soothing poultice to frayed souls. He straightens, but not with anger. "Gin is a *Justitian*. She can no more give up being one than you can change the color of your skin by thinking it done. The bond is irreversible. We have to learn to accept the inevitable if we wish to move forward."

Eloise, the deep thought guru.

Giving her a narrowed glare, T removes her hand, placing it on her leg and stands. "Just 'cause you accept something as is, don't mean you have to like it."

He wraps me in a quick hug before storming out of the room. Eloise sighs.

"Sorry." I pat her shoulder. "You tried. Thank you

again for saving me."

"It was my pleasure, Gin. I only wish...never mind."

"You have the hots for my twin, don't you?"

Red tinges her cheeks. Bingo. As if I didn't already know.

"We shouldn't discuss this."

"Just tell him how you feel. He likes you too."

She stands, the red tinge on her face turning into a deep rose. "I am most glad you are better, Gin. I must be going, but will visit you again, I'm sure."

With a wave of her hand, she vanishes into a portal.

Avoidance seems to be a theme tonight.

My stomach decides to rumble, reminding me it's been empty for more than a day. Thank you, Rahab. I walk out of my bedroom toward the kitchen, relieved to see the Agency cleanup crew has been hard at work. Not a scratch, tear or hole in the place. Amazing what a group of mages and some spells can accomplish.

T stands at the window staring into the darkened street. Yep, I definitely slept for an entire day. A quick glance at the clock shows it to be six-thirty.

"You okay?"

T turns to me, leaning against the cabinet. "You almost died."

"Eloise fixed me."

"Yeah, but what if she couldn't? What if she wasn't available? You can't die on me."

"Trust me, I don't want to die on you. But fighting demons is my job."

"Then I'm going to learn to be a ghost talker."

"You've said that before."

"Didn't really mean it before." A hint of red splashes his cheeks as his lips twitch. "Was a way to get closer to Eloise."

Ah-ha! My suspicion proved correct. "What changed your mind?"

"Both she and Smythe said ghost talkers can control ghosts to fight demons. All I have to do is learn how, then I can help you and you won't get hurt."

I smile. From my heart to my lips. I love my twin, he's the best, but… "I can't let you do something where you could be hurt."

"Like I don't feel the same way about you?"

Pot, kettle, Gin. Heat touches my cheeks. "Yeah, well. I can say that."

"Uh-huh. And so can I." He crosses his arms. "How hard can it be?" His jaw tenses as his gaze grows distant. Memories. Always with the memories even when we wish they would vanish into the mists of time never to return.

"Ever since—" I wave a hand between us. He doesn't need me to say the words to remember the day we killed our father, buried his body in a fresh grave and used a ghost's help to do the deed. The evil of that particular ghost freaked T out from ever wanting to talk to another spirit. "—that day, you swore off talking to ghosts. Hell, you even poured salt around our windows and doors."

"Lot of good it did. Blake still came in."

I swallow at the mention of my dead friend and lover. Pain punches me in the chest, lighter than normal, but still a reminder of my loss.

"Probably because we used the doors and windows. But that's not the point. The point is you fear what a ghost might say." At his expression from the word "fear" I hurry to finish the rest of my thought. "You haven't wanted to change before and it's okay, I understand, really I do, but you can't go against your sense of self-preservation, or whatever, to feel like you're coming to my rescue. I don't want you hurt by another evil ghost."

He drops his arms, pressing his lips together for a moment. "They aren't all bad, you know. Ghosts. Some of them are helpful. Most aren't evil."

"You just found the one that was."

"Yeah." He runs a hand over his head, his buzzed short, brown hair not moving. "Did what had to be done, but damn, it was one scary fucker. It's time for me to get over myself. They aren't all evil. And people like me, true ghost talkers, not mediums, are rare. I can help fight demons. Hell, if I learn enough control, I can take out a demon. Send its ass back to burn."

"But not kill him. Or her. Ghosts can't kill a demon." I hold up my wrist, give the *justitia* a shake. "Only this can."

"Maybe not, but they can damage 'em all the same."

I stare into his eyes, seeing nothing except determination. Which means no matter what I say, no matter how hard I argue against it, nothing I say will change his mind. He wants to learn to control ghosts, to convince the little see-through buggers do his bidding. To make a difference.

Can't blame him there. I want to make a difference too.

"Do they train you? Or throw you into the field and hope for the best?"

One side of his mouth quirks. "Both, sorta. There's not been a ghost talker at the Agency in a while, so no one who can personally train me. But there are plenty of books, or so Eloise says."

"What does Smythe say?"

"He doesn't seem as familiar with it as she does."

I'm learning Smythe doesn't know as much as I thought. Which doesn't mean he's stupid, except when it comes to Donny.

A potent mix of anger and shame roils through my chest as I draw in a deep breath. Donny is not the topic of this convo; T is, so I need to focus on my twin and not the football star I killed. Hard to do when grief sucker punches me with no warning.

T's brow furrows. Uh-oh, I took too long to answer.

"You okay?"

"Yeah, yeah. My mind took a rabbit path. Anyway, back to you. When do you start hitting the books?" Who would've thought my twin would become a study-aholic?

T answers after a pause. "As soon as Eloise can bring them to me."

Little warning bells echo in my brain. "Wait. What do you mean, when she brings them to you? Aren't you going to go to the Agency's library and study?"

He shrugs. "I'm telling you what she told me. She'll bring the books here."

"Does the Agency know she asked you to become a ghost talker?"

"I suppose. Why?"

Now it's my turn for a shrug. "It seems a little odd to me. When I first became a *Justitian,* Smythe brought

96

me in to meet his father, the leader of the mages. Would've thought they'd do the same with you."

T crosses his arms, narrows his eyes. "Yeah. That makes sense. So what's she playing at?"

"Might not be anything. Bringing the books to my place might be the way they operate for ghost talkers, I have no idea. Just saying it seems a little hinky to me. Why don't you ask her?"

"Yeah, sure. She's supposed to come over tomorrow evening to chat after I get off work."

Work. I missed work today. As in, another mark against me. Until I started wearing the *justitia* I never had a write-up, a talking to, or anything derogatory about my performance on the job. And now? I seem to be getting write-ups every week. At this rate, I'll be out of a job.

Which would not be good on so many levels.

"You're gone, again, Gin."

T's voice turns my attention back to him.

"Sorry. Can't believe Ruth let you call in for me."

He grins. "I can be persuasive when needed."

I give him a hug. "Are you hungry?"

"Starving. Wanna try for steaks again?"

"Sure."

Chapter Ten

Hours later I sit on my bed, staring at my phone, playing a game. T is in bed, but due to a twenty-four-hour healing session I'm awake and ready to go. Unfortunately, going somewhere is not an option. Hence the game.

Which does nothing to soothe my frazzled mind.

For the first time all week, Donny's death ranks as the least of my worries. Normally, I'd agree it was a good thing to no longer be focused on my involvement in his early demise. However, with T's little ghost talker announcement, my mind whirls like an out-of-control dervish.

Was my twin really going to hop on the Agency's bandwagon of demon killing expertise? Or was he going all out to impress the girl, a.k.a Eloise? Even asleep, his mind is impervious to my telepathic attempts.

"Leave it all behind. Take my hand."

The deep voice from inside my room jerks my head up from where I stare at my phone. The dream man, who I now know to be a despair demon, stands against the wall, outline fuzzy like a hazy spirit come for a visit. My breath hitches as my body freezes in a vain attempt to hide. As if my statue-like posture renders me invisible to a demon who can project itself inside my mind. Forcing myself to move, I shake the *justitia*, but the damn thing won't turn into a sword.

Really? Come on. There's a freaking demon in my room!

The thing performs the equivalent of a shrug along my nerves. *No demon. No sword.*

Great. I'm on my own.

Swallowing a hunk of fear disguised as a dry mouth, I glare at the fuzzy demon. Because glaring makes one look tough.

Fake it until you make it.

"You aren't real." I lower my phone to the bed one inch at a time, hoping the slow speed will avoid him noticing the movement.

Which, of course, he's going to notice since his attention focuses on me with the hyper-acuity of a predator to its prey.

All these thoughts rush through my mind in the time it takes the demon to blink in surprise at my announcement. Puzzlement covers his face as he fumbles for a comeback.

"Don't be ridiculous. I'm as real as you." He holds out his hand. "My name is Perdix. Come to me. I will give you rest."

I fail to stop the eye roll. "Drop the act, buster. I'm on to you." I point a finger at him. "Why don't you tell me where you're at so we can meet one on one? Then we'll see who gives who rest."

Pushing off the wall, he glares at me while taking a step forward. "I'm powerful. You will treat me with respect."

Oh come on. If demons want respect they need to come up with some better lines.

"Respect's earned. You don't have it. Come on, tell

me where you're really at. Next door? Down the street? Outside my window? You can tell me." I stretch my hand out, palm up, and waggle my fingers in a come-to-me wave.

He takes a step closer, but I'm not fooled. He's not about to grab my hand. Nor do I really want him to, so I drop my hand to my lap. Judging from his narrowed eyes, he's more likely to hit me than clasp palms. He circles to the side of the bed, his gaze dropping from my face to my neck, brows furrowed.

He gestures toward my neck. "Pull back your hair."

"Excuse me?" The request is a new one for a demon.

"Pull back your hair."

What the hell? I do as he asks, grabbing my hair with one hand. It's not like he can go all vampire and bite me. He's not physically present in the room, he's merely a projection.

I hope.

He stares a bit too long at my neck. Okay. Maybe he can bite me. I drop my hair, scoot toward the other side of the bed.

"You carry his mark." He snarls.

Now it's my turn for the surprised face. "You recognize Zagan's mark?"

When I first became a *Justitian* and met Zagan, the freakin' demon marked me as his with a small black tattoo on my neck close to my hairline. For any other human, it would mean becoming a servant of the demon. For me, it's just a mark.

Or so I've convinced myself.

"You are his servant." Perdix grins. "Until I kill you."

"You can't. Not as you are now." I gesture to his non-corporeal body.

He raises a brow, shooting me a condescending look. "Are you so stupid to think I'm always in this form? When we meet, I will kill you."

"Bring it, bud. Hey, why don't you tell me where you are now so you don't have to wait."

"You are too well protected." He sneers. "By a filthy half-breed. We will meet again."

After uttering his B-movie line, Perdix vanishes without a sound, leaving behind more questions along with a pounding heart and adrenaline rush.

I still don't know where he's located or how he sends out his spirit or whatever to assault unsuspecting victims. And what the hell did he mean I'm too well protected? By Zagan? By a sleeping T? Or did Smythe demon-proof the house? And who was the filthy half-breed? Half-breed of what?

Who was he referring to? Definitely not T. While one could consider our father a mongrel, he was human. Smythe? Nope, same thing. Human parents. Zagan? Were demons half-breeds? Even if they were, I'm not convinced Zagan currently protects me. Sure, I wear his mark, but the last time I saw the demon he was mad enough to incinerate me so I highly doubt he threw some protective mojo my way.

Who else would protect me?

One way to find out.

I close my eyes, tapping into the entity lying along my nerves. A bright purple glow appears in my mind.

Who was the demon referring to? Who's the half-breed?

A long pause.

Abomination. Other.

Abomination? Other? What the hell do you mean?

Not hell. Wrong.

Wrong? What's wrong?

Abomination.

Who is an abomination?

Half-breed.

Yeah. This conversation is going nowhere fast. Who was a half-breed abomination? What made them an abomination? Their half-breed status?

Geez Louise, would I ever have answers or only more questions?

Words pop into my mind, courtesy of my circuitous conversation-making *justitia*. *Angel-human abomination.*

My eyes snap open. *Angels?*

Huh, demons exist. Why not angels?

I get the impression the *justitia* snorts. Other than its disdain, silence reigns.

And the conversation, if one could call it such, ends. Despite my prods and requests, the *justitia* clams up, refusing more information. Even though the damn thing knows good and well who the angel-human abomination is.

The next Agency member who shows up at my house will get asked the same question: who the hell is my *justitia* calling an abomination?

****

I finally fall asleep around four in the morning, only to be awakened at eight by thudding footsteps in the kitchen. Never a good way to wake. My heart races in an uneven rhythm until I smell the distinct aroma of sizzling bacon and brewing coffee. Since T has to be at work by seven, the only other person who would be making me breakfast would be Smythe. Unless a benevolent alien landed in my kitchen and decided to cook for me.

Yeah, and those chances are zilch.

What was Smythe doing in my house? Besides the obvious? Wasn't he pissed at me? Felt betrayed by me? Behaving like an ass?

Yep, yep, and yep.

Nothing to it but to drag myself out of bed.

After a quick shower and clothes change, I follow the delicious aroma into the kitchen. Smythe stands at the stove scrambling eggs, the wooden spoon hitting with a soft *thud-thud-thud* against the side of the pan.

My heart beats a staccato rhythm as I draw in a deep breath. *Calm, Gin, calm. Do not go nuclear on his ass. He's making you breakfast.*

I draw in another deep breath. Coffee and breakfast first. Argue later.

"Hey." See? I can sound calm and collected. Fake it until you make it. At my greeting, he turns. Swallows.

"Hey."

"Whatcha doing?"

He gives me a quick brow raise. "Cooking breakfast."

"I mean besides the obvious."

A long pause ensues as he looks at the ground, punctuated by the crackle of sizzling bacon and the hiss of gas under the pans.

Several deep breaths later, his gaze meets mine. "I'm sorry."

I blink a couple of times. Well, you don't hear him saying those words every day. So much for coffee and breakfast first. I should be happy about it. Instead, while relief eases through my veins, it's swamped by a large dose of righteous indignation.

Apparently I can't take an apology.

"Thank you." If he's going to man up and apologize, the least I can do is thank him. No matter what I really feel. "What brought this on?"

His gaze flicks to the ground, only to return to mine. "I read the cleanup crew's report on the matter."

I can't stop my brows, or my voice, from rising. "And you believed them when you wouldn't believe me?"

"I'm sorry."

Don't be a bitch, Gin. Don't be a bitch.

I draw in a deep breath through my nose. Hold it for a ten count then blow it out while relaxing my clenched fists.

"So you finally believe me?"

"I do." He turns off the burner under the eggs. "I should've known you wouldn't kiss him willingly. But in all fairness, you kept defending him against all odds."

Anger drains from my body. While his previous attitude was wrong, I did continue to defend Donny long past the time I should've faced the obvious facts. My gaze drops to the floor for a second, the tone of my voice soft to cover a wrong. I should've seen through Donny. But…

"I didn't want him to be guilty. He seemed…nice."

"Seriously?" Smythe waves a hand. "Whatever. He wasn't and you now know."

"Yeah. I do." I clear the lump of guilt from my throat. "He didn't deserve to die though."

"True that. And you didn't deserve for me to walk out and leave you to fight Rahab alone. When I saw the two of you, all I could think of was"—he shakes his head as if clearing an old memory—"well, I shouldn't have let jealousy blind me to what was going on."

His gaze strokes across my frayed spirit, soothing the unraveled ends, pulling me into his spell. But I don't want to fall again. I'm not ready to fall again. As petty as it seems, I'm not done being mad.

"I'm not sure if I'm ready to forgive you."

"Fair enough." He twists off the burner under the bacon. "Breakfast is ready."

Because nothing erases guilt and shame like a good breakfast.

I grab two plates, hand him one and fill mine with bacon and egg goodness. After pouring myself an extra-large mug of coffee, I sit across from Smythe at the table. Except for forks clicking against the plates, silence reigns.

He did what I wanted: apologized. So why do I still feel upset?

Probably because it takes awhile to get over the man you cared about accusing you of cheating on him. While I can't control what I feel, I can act like an adult instead of a petty child.

Because rising above things is what adults do. Even when they'd rather throw hot coffee on a person and scream at the top of their lungs.

"The man from my dreams, the despair demon, has a name: Perdix. I know this because visited me again last night." Might as well talk about demons. It beats sitting in silence wanting to act like an uber bitch.

Smythe coughs, choking on a piece of egg. "Come

again?"

"The despair demon visited me last night. Or his projection visited me. Tried to get me to come to him. As if I would. Then he saw Zagan's symbol," I point to my neck, as if Smythe forgot about the mark, "said he was going to kill me but couldn't right then because I was too well protected. Then he vanished."

"He knows you won't fall for his charms."

"Charms?" I snort. "Whatever. Anyway, he said my protector was a filthy half-breed so I asked the *justitia* what he meant by a half-breed. Catch this, it said the half-breed was an angel-human abomination. Wanna let me in on who the hell it is? Because it isn't you. Or T. Or Zagan. And there wasn't anyone else offering me protection."

Bacon hangs from Smythe's fingers, paused halfway between his plate and his mouth. He blinks several times at me as the bacon falls onto his plate, his face draining of color.

Ah-ha. He knows who my *justitia* meant.

He clears his throat. "How did your *justitia* know?"

"Wouldn't say. The thing talks oddly and in a circle. Who is it?"

"It's not my place to say." The color returns to his cheeks as he grabs his dropped piece of bacon and pops it into his mouth.

"Aw, come on."

"No."

"Seriously?"

"Seriously."

Mages and their damned secrets. "Then how do I find out about my mysterious hybrid protector?"

"You don't. Just know you've been protected. It

106

doesn't happen to everyone."

"Fine. Then how did they protect me? If there's a spell to protect from demons, then why don't they cast it over humankind? Show the demons who's boss?"

"That's not how it works. Did Perdix give you a clue where he was projecting from?"

As someone who changes topics whenever a question hits too close to home, I recognize a topic avoidance when I see one. And I know my mentor. If he won't disclose something, no amount of wheedling will get it out of him. Best thing to do is go along with his topic change and try again later.

I will learn who the heck the angel-human abomination is. And how they managed to protect me.

Demons and angels. Until I took this job, I didn't believe either existed.

"The demon didn't answer my question regarding his whereabouts. Rather like you're doing."

Good thing frosty glares from Smythe fail to make me squirm.

"He has to be close. A despair demon can't project from too far. About the distance of a block or two according to the research I did."

"What else did your research turn up about despair demons?"

"They don't normally cause a person to commit suicide. While they will project themselves to a person who is dying and can feed across distances through their projection, they normally appear in the flesh to feed. On someone who has already made the choice. This is one of the few instances I could find of one projecting to victims who are sad and upset but not depressed. Not sure why this is happening."

That makes two of us. Two unsure Agency employees trying to learn the rationale behind demon behavior.

No wonder we have no idea on the matter. Since when is demon behavior rational?

I clear my throat. "You talked before of demon leaders. Maybe leaders have extra abilities."

"Or a despair demon hasn't tried to kill this many people at once so it has never been noted in the history books."

"Okay. If that's the case, why is he doing it now? What does he gain?"

Smythe shrugs. "What all demons gain, I suppose. A boost in power."

"Yeah, okay. But why? Why now? What's going on now to make this demon need a power boost?"

"Something in Hell?"

"Hell yeah!" I slap the table with a laugh while Smythe rolls his eyes.

"Be serious. Something could be going on in Hell. Why don't you ask Zagan?"

"Because he's no longer speaking to me."

A wrinkle appears between Smythe's brows. "Did you tell me this?"

"Not the whole story." My breath hitches. Telling Smythe about Zagan is like pulling a scab from a wound. My words escape in a jumbled rush. "He got mad the night I killed Donny. Said his red energy would have killed Rahab, but I wasted it on blasting those minions who shot up the Agency at that mandatory meeting. He didn't buy the argument that saving mages was a good deal. Something about demons and mages not liking each other? Yeah.

Anyway. He called me a loser and portaled away. Haven't seen him since."

I neglect to mention how much this bothers me. How I feel bereft without Zagan's occasional presence. How—either because of the *justitia* or some personal deficiency—he's become somewhat of a friend. Who would've thought I'd grow accustomed to visiting with a demon. Definitely not Smythe.

And since my mentor just apologized and is trying to act like we're all good, I'll cut him some slack by conveniently forgetting to mention my wayward feelings. Even if a hollow, painful ache takes up residence in my chest at the thought of the absent demon.

"I guess that's a good thing." Smythe leans back in his chair, his fingers drumming against his jean-clad leg. "But it's still strange. He marked you. He thinks of you as his servant."

"No, he thinks of me as his friend. Or the *justitia* as his friend. Or maybe he thinks we're one and the same. Me and the *justitia*." At Smythe's brow-raised expression, I clamp my lips together to stop rambling.

After a two second pause, he continues. "As I was saying, you wear his mark. Humans who wear a demon's mark are the demon's servant. And yet, you aren't. Maybe he grew tired of not being able to turn you and gave up. You should be thankful."

So why wasn't I?

Chapter Eleven

After breakfast, we sit at the kitchen table, me with the newspaper and a cup of coffee and Smythe with his ever-present laptop. Much to my surprise, Smythe lets me drink three cups of coffee without complaining about my habit. Good thing too, seeing how I need it to wake up. Despite a kickass healing combined with sleeping for a day, only four hours of rest the night before left me groggy. You would've thought I'd be awake and ready to catch a demon, but nope, I'd rather catch another four hours of z's.

Newspaper rustles as I flip the page. Fingers *tap-tap-tap* against keys. Smythe and his love for his laptop. I swear, the man is never far from technology.

The tapping stops. I look up from the cooking article to see Smythe staring at me.

"What?"

"I have good news. I discovered how Samantha paid those minions who tried to kill you."

When I first started this gig, Samantha—a blonde-bitch mage—fooled me into going with her to fight minions. Sure, there were minions, but only because she hired them to kill me.

Smythe's dad, David, believed her story over mine so Smythe has been hunting for how she paid off the minions. He discovered a bank transfer from her account to another, but needed to further flesh out the details. I guess he found the trail.

A "gotcha, bitch" smile turns my lips. "You were still looking?"

His gaze flicks to his laptop and back to mine. "I found it this morning. Right in front of me. It took me a while to find the account's owner who received the transfer. One Lars Sigmundson. A little more research including pictures and Lars isn't really Lars. Try Jezebeth."

Cold rushes through me, replaced by heat. Jezebeth killed Blake. At least I killed the demon bitch.

And now we have proof Samantha paid the demon to use her minions to kill me.

"Why would she pay minions to off me?" Why would Samantha hate me enough to hire minions to kill me? Samantha is a mage. A mage. Mages fight demons, not hire them to kill newbie *Justitians*.

"It gets worse." He shoves the laptop out of the way and leans forward, elbows on the table. "The money in Samantha's account came as a single deposit from the Agency. It looks like she was the middleman. Or woman as the case may be."

I blink. Once, twice. As if the action will make the news improve.

It doesn't. I knew most people at the Agency agreed with Samantha about me not deserving to wear the *justitia* because I wasn't born into the life, but I didn't think they hated me enough to kill me.

"Are you sure? I mean, are you sure it's not a coincidence? Like they were going to pay her anyway and she used her paycheck to finance a murder?" Yes, Samantha was a bitch, thought I was white trash, and didn't think me worthy to wear the *justitia*.

I also suspect she still had a thing for Smythe. All of which made her anger toward me somewhat understandable. But to learn the Agency, my employer, tried to have me killed without even letting me learn my job, hurt. I knew they didn't like me, maybe even agreed with Samantha's no-good, white-trash conclusion, but to have me killed?

I knew the Agency was up to no good. Just didn't realize their 'no good' was directed at me.

"It's not a coincidence." Anger snaps around Smythe, flashes in the depths of his eyes. "Her paycheck isn't anywhere close to the amount deposited."

"So not only does someone at the Agency want me dead, they also refuse to pay me when they pay others?" Really, what was wrong with me? I should be focusing on the "someone wanting me dead" part of this conversation and instead I'm pissed at the lack of income in this gig. If I'm dead, the income, or lack thereof, won't matter.

Breathe in and out, in and out.

"All mages get paid."

"And *Justitians* don't?" So much for calming effects of deep breaths. "What the hell? We're the ones who can permanently put the hurt on a demon."

He shrugs. "The point here is someone wants you dead."

Good point. Maybe I should get off my tirade and focus on the more pressing issue of the Agency gunning for my death.

"Why? What did I do to piss someone off that much?" I shake my wrist, rattling the silver links of my *justitia*. "Is this the reason? You'd think they'd be happy someone was wearing the bracelet instead of letting it sit in a magical vault gathering dust."

"You'd think. I don't know. The routing number on the deposit was the same as all her paychecks."

"Who has access to tell finance to pay her extra?"

Smythe's jaw tenses. Yeah. I don't need him to speak the words. His father has access. But David's not who he says.

"Chuck Tweedy."

The head of the Agency. The big boss. I've only met him once, seen him twice, and neither time was enjoyable. But both times were after Samantha put a hit on me.

"Why would he want me dead?"

"I'll do some more research on your *justitia*. I thought Samantha acted alone and hired the minions because she thought you weren't worthy of wearing a *justitia*. I didn't realize the Agency was behind it." He drums his fingers against the table, his face a mask of concentration. "If they wanted you dead badly enough to hire minions to kill you, then why haven't they struck again?"

"Maybe they realized I was tougher than I looked? Or I could actually perform as a *Justitian* and live up to the name?"

"Maybe. Or maybe they're biding their time for another opportunity."

Great. Just what I needed. A horde of mages out for blood. My blood. Heat electrifies my skin while turning my marrow to ice. I wrap my arms around my waist in an effort to stop shaking.

Smythe snaps his laptop closed. "I want to talk to Dad about this. I have proof of what Samantha did and proof the Agency was behind it. He would know who could have put her up to it."

I swallow and tense my annoying quivering muscles to speak without a tremor in my voice. "Not to be upsetting, but are you sure your dad isn't in on it? I mean, he hates my guts and refused to believe you when you told him of Samantha's duplicity."

Smythe negates my theory with a head shake. "He can be an ass. But why would he want you dead? There're plenty of people he doesn't like—"

No big surprise there. Plenty of people who don't like him either, I imagine.

"—but it doesn't mean he wants them dead. Or would go to the trouble of killing them. No, Dad doesn't have anything to do with this. If we want to learn who could, then we need to talk to him."

"We?" My voice escapes in a high-pitched tone.

"You should be there. You're the one she tried to kill."

I shoot him a go-to-hell glare. He raises a brow. I hate it when he makes a good point. Especially when his good point involves me making a trip to the Agency.

"Fine."

Just what I wanted to do. Take a trip to the Agency and talk to David. What started off as a great day gets worse by the minute.

Chapter Twelve

We portal into the white landing room of the Agency. The scent of lavender tickles my nose, eliciting a sneeze. A row of teenage mages-in-training glance up from where they sit staring at computer screens, monitoring demon appearances on Earth. Or trying to. In theory, this line of young mages can stop a demon from invading the Agency's building. In reality, I doubt they can do much more than wear a shocked expression when an incoming demon pounds them into dust.

One of them offers me a tissue, a change from their usual ignore the mage and *Justitian* arrivals. I take the proffered tissue, offer my thanks, and follow Smythe into the hall.

The golden chandeliered hall. Clearly the Agency has no problem bringing in the big bucks. Wait. Why do they have so much money? Good investments? Or shady dealings?

I knew they were filthy rich, but until now failed to ask myself, Smythe, or anyone else who'd listen, how they came to roll in the dough.

Smythe leads us to the elevator and hits the UP button.

In the privacy of the elevator, I ask him the question I should've asked when I first started working this gig.

"How does the Agency get its money?"

"Investments." He shrugs in a no big deal way. "We've been around for almost as long as the *justitias*. Plenty of time to invest in a wide variety of things. Save a couple of antiquities, sell them off in the future and you have a super-sized bank account."

Makes sense. Then why do I doubt it's the reason behind the wealth?

"You sure about that?"

"Of course. What else could it be?"

The elevator arrives at the top floor, its gentle ding interrupting my brow-raised say-what expression. Once the doors slide open, I turn to Smythe.

"I'm learning my original suspicion of the Agency was correct: things are shady as hell around here."

Smythe stares at me, silence gathering around us as we step out of the elevator into the anteroom leading to the penthouse suit.

"Things might be shady now, but there's no way the money came from anything but investments or selling off antiques kept for that specific purpose. I've seen their investment accounts." His tone expresses a confidence I fail to feel. "If it makes you feel better, we can ask Dad about it."

Yeah, like David's going to reveal the truth. But "mmm" is all I say as I trail behind my mentor to David's door.

Smythe knocks on the door. "Dad? You home?"

Footsteps, dulled through the door, draw near. Locks click. I draw in a breath. David opens the door. A grin starts to turn his lips as he looks at his son. Until he sees me. All remnants of happiness disappear.

"What is it?" The gruffness of his voice raises my hackles.

"May we come in? We need to talk."

David steps back, pulling the door wide. His icy glare burns a hole between my shoulder blades as I walk past him.

Always nice to know people enjoy my company.

Snark aside, did he dislike me enough to hire Samantha to kill me?

The door clicks into place, sealing us inside the posh penthouse. Tension swirls around the room, thick as congealing blood.

My *justitia* shoots a round of puzzlement along my nerves, the silver links rattling with confusion.

Demon?

Don't be ridiculous. We're at the Agency.

Demon. This time its tone conveys conviction. But it remains in bracelet form.

Thank goodness.

Puzzlement while in the Agency appears to be the thing's emotion of choice. I blame it on the low-buzzing white noise, a side effect of spells coating the building from nosy outsiders. White noise makes me nervous, why wouldn't it my bracelet?

David gestures for us to sit on an overstuffed leather sofa, while he perches on the edge of an arm chair.

"You were wrong." Smythe starts the conversation in a way guaranteed to put his father on the defensive. Way to go, my guardian.

David raises a brow, his tone dry. "Really?"

"Samantha hired Jezebeth's minions to kill Gin." Smythe drops that revelation in the same manner most people state the weather is nice: calm and collected. "Remember how we told you about it right after it happened? Right after Gin became a *Justitian*? I traced the money. She's guilty."

David flinches. Not much, but enough for me to notice. His eyes flare for a second before he freezes, the rise and fall of his chest as he breathes the only indication he lives.

Then he clears his throat. "Are you sure?"

"Yep." Smythe nods. "A large payment hit her account a day before she transferred it out. It took me a while, but I found the account she transferred it to was owned by Jezebeth. Jezebeth's minions attacked Gin. Samantha's guilty."

Small white lines bracket David's mouth. "I need to see the proof."

"No problem." Smythe pulls out his ever-present laptop and boots it up. Once it comes on, he pulls up a document and turns the screen to his father.

David looks at the screen, his glacial blue eyes narrowing as he scrolls down the page.

"You've done a lot of work on this."

"She tried to kill Gin." The low tone of Smythe's voice rubs across my skin as his anger twines around the room. "Mages should not work with demons and minions. We fight them. Not hire them to kill *Justitians*."

David continues to stare at the screen. I keep my mouth shut. Telling him what needs to be done to Samantha tends to only make him mad. Or madder than he already is on a normal day. And there was the whole incidence of me using Zagan's demonic energy to fight the minions who attacked an Agency meeting.

I can guaran-damn-tee David hasn't forgotten about me shooting the demon's red energy from my palms. Or how I evaded his compulsion spell to tell him the truth about my new "ability." Of course, he doesn't know I evaded his spell; he thinks I told him the truth when I said I had no idea where the red energy came from or how I was able to use it.

Oh, who am I fooling? He knows I didn't tell the truth. He just can't figure out how I managed to lie or what I'm hiding.

All good reasons for me to sit quiet as a church mouse and take in the view of the Boston cityscape outside the wall of windows.

The man might be a dick, but you gotta give him credit for having a great view of the city.

David drums his fingers against his slate-gray pants, flicks his gaze from me to his son. "Who paid her?"

"The Agency. Same routing number as her paycheck."

"Fuck." David pinches the bridge of his nose.

"What are you going to do about it?"

A long pause ensues, long enough for the thought to cross my mind that David knew about Samantha's scheme to obliterate me and tried to cover it up. Maybe he was the one who paid her. Although he seems smarter than to send the payment from the Agency's finance department.

Now is definitely not the time to mention how I'd like in on a little Agency paycheck action.

Maybe another day.

"I'll talk to her."

"Talk to her?" So much for keeping my mouth shut. Both sets of male eyes focus on me. Who cares? David can't be serious. "What do you mean, talk to her?

Shouldn't you be arresting her? She. Tried. To. Kill. Me!"

Smythe pats my leg, non-verbal language for shut-the-hell-up-and-lower-your-voice.

I ignore him.

Red scorches a path across David's cheeks. "I said I'd take care of it."

"You said you'd talk to her. Not the same thing."

Smythe continues to pat my leg. Hate to tell him, but his attempt at calming me is not working.

"Dad, there's a problem in the Agency. Mages don't hire demons or minions. Ever. And yet a payment went out from the Agency finance to a mage to kill a *Justitian*. That's unheard of. You need to find out what's going on and put a stop to it. Before something worse happens."

Smythe shouldn't need to tell his father how to do his job. It's evident the Agency has issues. Major issues. David's attitude reinforces my belief he's behind it.

On the flip side, what would the boss of the mages gain by eliminating a *Justitian*? Especially one who's the last of her ancestral line? Unless that was the whole goal. But why would they want that to happen? Nothing about this makes sense.

Except Samantha truly is a bitch.

"Samantha's a good mage. One of our best. I want to hear her side of the story before we"—David shoots me a glare, while clearing his throat—"arrest her."

"You did that once." I return his glare with one of my own. "And sided with her. What's changed?"

"Proof." He waves a hand at the laptop. "What you told me before was only hearsay."

Only Smythe's palm on my thigh stops me from leaping off the sofa. Hearsay? Clearly the man is bonkers.

"You both are missing the bigger picture." David raises a brow as his son speaks. "Samantha paid off the minions, but it's obvious she was told to do so by someone at the Agency. Someone not smart enough to hide the cash trail, but someone higher up." He swallows, glances down before meeting David's gaze. "Was it you?"

David blinks, his mouth sliding open before closing. "Goddamn it son, I can't believe you'd ask that question."

Okay, neither can I. I always thought Smythe trusted his father to be one of the good guys, despite all my evidence to the contrary. Shows me what I know.

Red tinges Smythe's cheeks. "It's a fair question. Few people have access to finance."

"Do you really think if I paid her off I'd use our own finance department to do so? Give me a little credit."

"Sorry. I had to ask." Smythe shrugs.

David runs a hand through his short, gray hair. "I did not pay her off. I believed her side of the story is all."

"Then who could pay her off?"

David repeats the hand through hair motion. "Several of us. But, why would they? Give me a reason."

"They hate me" is on the tip of my tongue, but I press my lips together to keep the comment inside. While I could pull the poor-poor-me card, this was bigger than me alone. Samantha barely knew me before trying to off me. Jealousy might go a long way in explaining her attitude toward me, but it wasn't everything. And since she was paid by the Agency, it means someone else wanted me dead.

David was the logical choice. But why would he want me dead? He acted like he didn't do it. Which didn't mean anything. I still don't trust the man. He doesn't like me. Would his dislike make him want to put me six feet under?

I'm beginning to lean toward no for the answer.

"Could it have something to do with her *justitia* and how it managed to escape from the security vault?" Smythe asks, lines of concentration etched across his face.

Could it? Could the entire reason the Agency hates my guts have nothing to do with me and everything to do with my *justitia*?

"It might sound like a good explanation, but still doesn't make sense." I glance at my guardian. "If you're in a demon war, why would you try to off one of the few people who can actually kill them? The *justitia* won't work for anyone but me, since the rest of my line is dead. Doesn't make sense." A thought hops to the front of my mind. "Unless you want the demons to win."

And not even the Agency—

David shifts before I finish my thought, drawing my attention to his wide-eyed, pale face. As if he was guilty. As if I hit a nerve.

As if I was correct.

His father's weight shift fails to pass Smythe's notice. He leans forward. "Something you want to tell us, Dad?"

Tension wraps the room at Smythe's cold tone. Could everything be explained by stating the Agency wants the demons to win this war? Was it really so simple?

Still doesn't explain why. After all, I can't imagine having demons in charge of Earth would be an improvement.

"Don't be ridiculous, son. Why would we want the damn demons to win? Do you know what would happen if they won? Do you know the havoc they'd wreak on Earth? Do you think we're fucking idiots?"

Good points. None of which erase the fact David's guilty as hell.

"You look like you know something." Give Smythe a proverbial bone and he'll gnaw at it until it cracks.

David glares while managing not to shift his weight. "Of course I know things. But not what you are implying. Why would you even think I'm guilty?"

Smythe raises a brow as I glance between the two men. What's gotten into him? This is the first indication I've seen he thinks his father deals in guilt and lies. I'm not complaining. Believing David guilty of something puts Smythe firmly in my corner. Stranger things have happened.

Silence descends as a round of stare-and-glare takes place. My gaze bounces from Smythe to his father, watching for a sign of who gives first. Neither does. Clearly, stubbornness runs in their family.

Red creeps across David's face, a sign of guilt or raw anger. Hard to tell which one.

"As I said, Dad, you look like you know more than you're letting on about Gin, her *justitia,* and who hired

Samantha to kill her."

"I'm not and you know it." David stands. "I've heard enough. I refuse to listen to these accusations. If you have nothing else to say, you can leave."

Smythe rises to his feet with the speed of stalking lion, his gaze remaining on his father. I shrink into the sofa as anger thickens the air.

"What did you do, Dad?"

Instead of an answer, David points at the door. "I said leave. I won't listen to your accusations."

Air buzzes around Smythe, around David, an impending storm full of energy flashes and crackles of ire. After what feels like an eternity while waiting for the shitstorm to dump on our heads, Smythe speaks.

"See you later, Dad. Come on, Gin."

He snaps shut his laptop, sticking it into his backpack before heading to the door.

David's glare sends shivers across my skin, making it crawl as if small ants march over my flesh. Smythe doesn't have to ask me twice to move my ass off the couch. I'm halfway to the door when David grabs my arm, flesh on flesh.

I let loose with a little squeak, unable to stop myself from jumping as his emotions flood my mind. Did he touch me skin-to-skin on purpose? He knows I'm an empath and usually avoids contact. Before I can do more than jump in surprise, Smythe stops, turns, and glares at David's hand on my arm. Instead of dropping my arm, like any sane person would do when faced with Smythe's glare, David pulls me toward him.

"I didn't say you could go."

Smythe steps toward his father, placing his hand on my shoulder. His voice rumbles in a low growl. "She comes with me."

"She's not telling me the truth."

It takes a liar to know a liar, eh David? But I keep the thought to myself, while twisting out of his grasp. I saw enough from his touch to know what he means.

"I already told you, David." I plant my feet, hands by my side, and give him my best nurse's glare. The one I use for ornery patients. "I don't know how I shot energy at those minions in the helicopter. It just happened."

"I don't believe you."

Neither do I, but it doesn't stop me from meeting his gaze. Hopefully, he can't see my heart pounding like a stampede behind my ribs.

"Well, you should." Smythe glares at his dad. "If she says she has no idea, then she has no idea. Come on, Gin. We need to leave."

He yanks open the door and I back through it, keeping one eye on David. His narrowed gaze trails across my skin as if looking for a path into my mind. I turn and quick-walk to the elevator, which opens as soon as Smythe hits the button.

Charles Tweedy, the head boss of the Agency steps out. My *justitia* shivers, the silver links trying to twist into a sword but failing.

Just like the last time I ran into the Big Boss. Just like it did earlier with David.

What is it about the Agency that bothers my *justitia*?

"Chuck." Smythe nods.

"Aidan." Chuck returns the nod. He raises a brow at me. "Gin Crawford, isn't it? Our mysterious *Justitian.*"

I slap a hand over the jittering bracelet. "Mr. Tweedy."

Greedy, greedy, greedy, the *justitia* chants in my head, loud enough to almost obliterate the Big Boss's next words.

"Call me Chuck. Everyone else does."

"Okay." I swallow. "Chuck." Can my voice sound any more high-pitched? Talk about a dead giveaway for how I really feel.

At least the damn *justitia* quiets. Although it continues to rattle against my wrist as if it wants to rub off my skin.

"I'm meeting with your father." He slaps a palm against Smythe's shoulder. "Gotta run."

"Later." My mentor raises a hand, but Chuck doesn't notice, his back already turned to us.

His leather loafers click against the marble tile of the foyer as he heads toward David's still open door. David gives us one more glare as he steps out of the way for his boss. We watch as the door snaps shut on their meeting.

As soon as he vanishes from view, my *justitia* resumes chanting, *greedy, greedy, greedy.*

Don't you mean, Tweedy, not greedy?

Greedy, greedy, greedy.

Annoying nonconversationalist. If it's going to talk, it might as well do so in actual sentences a human can understand.

"Gin?" Smythe pokes his head out of the elevator, one arm holding the door open, clearly waiting for me to get with the leaving program.

Right. No use in standing around in the foyer of the penthouse.

Chapter Thirteen

Once inside the elevator, I slump against the wall, tremors wracking my limbs. At least my body waited until I was away from David and Chuck before sinking into a trembling mess. No sense in looking weak before the big, bad mage or his big, bad boss.

I draw in a deep breath as I turn to Smythe. "Thanks for sticking up for me."

"He tried to compel you to tell him how you shot down those minions." His eyes narrow. "Didn't think you wanted to spill your guts."

"Good deduction. What do you think he knows? Do you think he tried to have me killed?"

"No, I don't think he did." His lips flatten as he stares at the elevator buttons. "But he knows more than he's letting on. I bet he knows who did it and doesn't want to say."

"Okay, but it still doesn't explain why. I thought Samantha wanted me dead because she had a raging case of jealousy. But—"

His gaze meets mine, furrowed brows highlighting blue eyes. "Jealousy?"

I look at the corner of the elevator, where the ceiling meets the wall, and clear my throat. "She likes you. Not that it matters—"

"What? We're no longer like that."

Heat slaps my cheeks as I meet his wide-eyed WTF

gaze. I wave my hand in a never mind gesture.

"Anyway, as I was saying—"

"No, back up. You really thought she was jealous of you because you and I work together and she still had a thing for me?"

I shrug, hoping the lighting prohibits him from noticing my apparently red face. It could happen. "It was a valid theory. You've got to admit, she hates my guts, and claiming I'm not good enough to wear the *justitia* is only half of it. No one can care that much about my background."

His look morphs from surprised to get-real. "Of course they can. But you're right, Samantha's issues aren't the only thing going on here. Still can't believe you thought she was jealous of you."

Once again, heat splashes my cheeks, but I verbally plod forward. "As I was saying when so rudely interrupted, jealousy and not thinking I'm good enough to wear the *justitia* only get you so far. I'm learning it's more than just me. I now think it has to do with my *justitia*."

"Yeah, that's my thought too. Finding the reason is going to be harder than finding out your past."

The elevator dings and we step into the hall. Instead of continuing our conversation, we silently agree to not speak of it until we get back to my place. At least that's my assumption for why Smythe strides down the hall to the landing room without saying a word.

Maybe he's tired of my company.

Nah. The building has ears in the form of eavesdropping devices or magical spells that channel all conversations to a computer for later review.

Or so I imagine. The computer, that is.

I follow Smythe into the lavender scented white-walled landing room and through a portal to my bacon, egg, and coffee scented kitchen. Ah, home.

Smythe walks into the living room where he resumes his feet-on-the-coffee-table pose, laptop open on his thighs.

"Want something to drink?" I lean against the wall, watching his fingers dance a jig across the keyboard, wishing they were dancing across my skin.

So much for remaining mad at him. The longer I'm around him, the more pieces of my anger dissipate.

His words snap me back to reality.

"Water, please. Or tea if you have it. But not the sweet crap you Texans like."

Okay, then. No sweet tea. Water it is.

After handing him a glass full of ice water, I plop on the sofa beside him, peering at the screen. A map of my neighborhood fills the page. What's he looking at now?

"You're not pulling up anything to do with my *justitia* or why the Agency wants me dead." I point at the map.

"True. Those things are going to take longer than a day to uncover. So I decided to work on where Perdix might be hanging out. He must be someplace nearby or else he wouldn't have been able to project to you. I'm looking at houses for sale. If they're empty, he might have moved in."

"What about the other victims? Have you looked in their neighborhoods?"

"No. Thought I'd start here since this was the last place he was. I looked earlier and no more suicides have been reported, so it appears he's moved on."

"You mean he's moved on to my neighborhood." A shot of ice rushes down my spine.

Smythe nods. "Since no more suicides have been reported and you saw him recently, your neighborhood is a likely place to search."

Great. Just what I wanted, a not-so-friendly neighborhood demon. Talk about an event to drop real estate prices.

"What did you find?"

"Still looking."

He takes a sip of water, then expands the map to street view in front of a house.

"You recognize this house?" He points at the screen.

I shake my head. "Not really. It's not too far from me, though."

"And it meets the criteria of being close and for sale. Want to go check it out?"

"Just because it's for sale doesn't mean it's empty."

His raised brow stare indicates he doubts my intelligence.

"What? Like I said, it doesn't mean the house is empty."

One corner of his mouth twitches. He points at the screen.

"We can land on the side of the house. It should be obscured from the street. Are you ready to check it out?"

Time to catch me a demon. Damn straight I'm ready to check it out.

"We still don't know why he killed so many people

all at once."

Smythe puts his glass on the coffee table, sets the laptop beside it, and stands. "Like I said, maybe he's gathering strength."

"Yeah, yeah, but we don't know that for sure. Although it makes a hell of a lot of sense. Hell of a lot. Get it?" I grin.

He closes his eyes, shakes his head.

"Seriously. You really think something is going on in Hell to make Perdix go on a killing spree?"

Smythe shrugs. "It's a logical guess."

"You mean like a demon war? From what little I know, it seems like demon infighting is a common occurrence." Clearly, I need to pay more attention to Demonology 101.

Oh, right. No wonder I'm clueless. The class doesn't exist.

"It's my best guess. When we catch him, you can ask him before you kill him."

"Right. Because I'm now Gin the interrogator, dishing up conversation with my slicing and dicing." I roll my eyes.

Smythe's lips twitch as he huffs. "Ready?"

He mutters his portal forming words, opening a passageway to the in-between in my living room. Warm air billows out, luring the unsuspecting traveler to expect beach-like weather on the inside. Once we step into its depths, the air turns brittle cold, stealing the breath from my lungs.

We arrive on the side of the house, me cold and trembling while Smythe acts like air the temperature of space is equivalent to the warmth of a Texas autumn.

He peeks in a window, while I shake my hands. At

least the October air is pleasant, in the mid-sixties with partial sun.

"Damn it. Looks like people still live here."

I step beside him, putting my nose close to the glass to see inside. "Looks staged to me."

"Staged?" His furrowed brow clues me in he's apparently never been shopping for houses. Or seen home shows on TV.

"You know, the owners make the place look like a model home because it attracts buyers."

His brow smoothes as he peers through the window. "You think we should go inside?"

"If you want to do a B&E, have at. I'll watch for police."

"And if the demon's inside?"

I take a deep breath, concentrating on the minion sensors in my eyes. No sense in breaking and entering for no reason. Minion sensors operational, I look through the window, releasing a relieved sigh.

"No minion trails. No evidence of a demon. What else you got?"

Smythe peers through the window again, brow furrowed. His face relaxes as he gives me a nod and half-grin. "Good catch. Let's see where the next empty house is."

He pulls out his phone while I try not to stare at him like he sprouted a third ear. My mentor, the man who consistently asks me to look for minion trails, who already knows the answer before I give it to him, forgot to check for demonic evidence?

Clearly, the conversation with his father bothered Smythe more than he lets on. He never, ever, ever forgets about the damn minion trails. I suppose learning there's a high probability your father made some shady deals would stress out anyone to the point they forgot the usual aspects of their job. Provided they cared about their old man. Which Smythe does, despite David's asshat tendencies.

"Two blocks over there's another house for sale." Smythe points at his phone.

"Lead the way, cowboy."

He raises a brow, his disdain with the nickname obvious without him uttering a word. Or at least uttering a word about "cowboy." His portal forming words don't count.

We land on the side of another house, behind a fungus-tinged, in dire need of a trim, photinia bush. I risk branches tearing my clothes and step behind the leafed behemoth to peek in a cracked window.

No staging furniture in this house. No furniture period. The place looks abandoned.

Smythe steps beside me, brushing off a black-spotted leaf from his arm. His eyes widen. Which, of course, makes me activate the minion sensors in my eyes before he can tell me to do it.

Bingo.

Red and orange trails darkened with a black haze encircle the room, traveling over every inch of the place, a clear indicator of demonic activity. Hopefully, it's the demon we're hunting and not a minion lair full of not-so-well-off minions. And the chances of a minion with no money?

I've learned it's more common to find a pearl in your oyster dinner.

Demons might be hellish to work for, but they make up for it in cold, hard cash.

Unlike the Agency.

Since my *justitia* remains as a bracelet, I assume the trails are remnants, no demonic presence currently on the premises.

"Did you see the trails?"

Smythe turns from the window, shooting me another raised brow, I'm-not-stupid expression.

"What? It's a viable question since you missed it the last time." I smile and elbow him in the ribs. "I guess this means we need to go inside."

"Definitely need to check it out. Make sure no one is in there."

"The place looks abandoned." I tap the window. "Do you think it's Perdix's hideout, or some random minion?"

"The black haze surrounding the trails indicate a demon, not a minion."

I look back at the trails, at what I noticed the first time, but failed to correlate to a demon. You'd think after several months working this gig I'd know the difference between demon and minion trails. Sometimes I wonder about myself.

"Right. I should've known that."

He shrugs in an "all good" manner. "Come on. We need to get in there and see what's going on."

He leads me into the backyard, the unlocked, chain-link-fence gate squeaking on its hinges like a tract from a horror movie. The backyard is as overgrown as the bushes along the side of the house. Tall grass interspersed with weeds gives the impression of a jungle hike. All we need is a machete.

Someone has beaten us to the back door. The thing hangs cracked open, one of its glass panes shattered.

Not deterred, Smythe steps inside, shoving the door wider with his elbow.

Demonic trails line this room, too. Thick and wide, the ribbons twine across the floor like streamers of blood. My nose wrinkles as I inhale a strong odor of mold.

"Yuck. Where is that stench coming from?" I wave a hand in front of my face, hoping the motion will dissipate the smell. It doesn't.

Smythe mirrors my expression, right down to the hand waving under his wrinkled nose. "Probably a water leak no one noticed."

"How can anyone live here?"

"They don't."

"You sure? A minion—"

"Still has a nose and wouldn't stay here long." He strides into the kitchen and points at something I can't see. Until I poke my head around the corner and notice the large, black stain spreading down the wall in the space where a refrigerator once stood, clearly originating from the water supply.

Double yuck. I can almost see the little spores of mold flying across the room to be sucked into my lungs where they would cause all sorts of hellish infections.

I clamp a hand over my nose and mouth and back out of the kitchen.

"Let's make this quick." Smythe strides past me, heading down the hall to the bedrooms.

Nothing but demonic trails. Since the trails usually dissipate after a day or so, and these appear bright, I conclude we just missed the walking evil.

"Looks fresh." Smythe gestures at a hazy black, red-orange trail.

"Yeah. We must've just missed him. At least we know where he's staying."

"We can either wait or come back."

"If you think I'm staying in this smelly house you have another think coming." I head toward the back door without waiting for his answer.

He follows, pulling the broken door shut behind us, then uses a spell to wipe his fingerprints off the knob. Good thing he's recovered enough from his shock to remember to erase evidence of us being at a breaking and entering site.

"I hoped the demon would be here." He stares at the door as if by glare alone he could summon Hell's emissary of death.

"We can come back." A thought wends through my mind. "Wait a minute. We can see minion and demon trails. Can demons or minions see mage and *Justitian* trails?"

He shakes his head. "Not to my knowledge. We'd have known if they could. We've been doing this for centuries."

Whew. "Okay. Then they won't know we've entered their domain and won't be waiting for us."

"That's the plan. Unless you wanted to sit out here and wait?"

"Nope. I'm pretty sure there's poison ivy out here. Just my luck I'd catch a case of it. Take me home, Jeeves."

He shakes his head, but does as I ask. The first thing I notice when we land in the kitchen is the sound of the TV. T should be at work, so who is in my house? Giving Smythe a quick there's-a-burglar-in-my-house look I head to the living room, my muscles coiled for a fight.

T sits on the couch, staring at "Ellen" on the screen. Ellen's on? Geez, I've completely lost track of time. No wonder T's home now. I take a step closer, about to say hi, when I notice sweat trickling down his pale face. His fingers ball into white, shaking fists.

While knowing no burglar snuck into my house to watch TV relaxes my ready-for-action nerves, seeing my twin in full on freak-out mode fails to lower my tension. Surely the show wasn't cause to look like he'd seen a ghost.

Oh, wait. Maybe he had.

"T?" I take a step toward my twin, Smythe right behind me. "T?"

No response.

I speed walk to my twin, touch his shoulder, startling him. "T, what's wrong?"

He turns to me eyes wide. "Our great-grandmother stopped by for a visit and you won't believe what she said."

Chapter Fourteen

"Is she still here?" I glance around the room, as if I can see a ghost. Wait a minute. I can if I touch my twin.

I grab T's hand, wrapping my fingers around his fist. A blurred figure appears between us and the TV. Female, shorter than me, maybe around five-two, and young. Clearly she died before reaching twenty. Her clothes remind me of what women wore in the late thirties, around the time of World War II.

She smiles at me, her eyes crinkling. Her eyes look like mine, like T's. Same shape. I can't tell the color on account of her being see-through. A little hard to tell the coloring of ghosts.

"What's she saying?" I ask.

"She's still here?" Smythe says at the same time.

I point to my great-grandmother. As if he can see her.

"Huh." Smythe nods, eyes squinting at the apparition.

T clears his throat, glances at me. "She told me her story. Our history."

"And?" Me.

"What was it?" Smythe.

We're going to win the award for simultaneous speaking.

The ghost gives a little finger wave and vanishes.

"Where'd she go?" I turn to T.

"She's gone?" Smythe looks between the both of us, his gaze landing on me before turning to my twin.

Color returns to T's face, sliding over the pale, returning his wide-eyed crazy-stare to his normal look. Not sure how he's going to handle being a ghost-talker when he can't even carry on a conversation with a dead relative without appearing like he's going into shock.

"I didn't ask where she's going or if she's coming back."

"Why not?"

T glares at me, the answer obvious in the press of his lips.

"How the hell are you going to be a ghost-talker if you can't talk to a ghost without freaking out?" It's a valid question, one I'm really curious about, one he needs to know the answer to before he ventures into this new job arena.

"I'll deal with it. It was more what she said than the fact she's a ghost."

"What was so shocking?" Smythe asks. "And how did she find you? Why now? Why hadn't she tried to contact you before?"

Leave it to my mentor to ask questions that trump mine in importance. Not like peppering T with questions is a contest.

A fine wrinkle between T's eyes appears only to disappear a second later. He shrugs. "She didn't see the need to get in touch until Gin started wearing the bracelet. Ghosts don't tell time like we do. She thought Gin just started wearing the *justitia*, like last week. So in her mind she was Johnny-on-the-spot to pop in and say hi. I was sitting here watching TV when she appeared." A splash of red tints his cheeks. "I took down the ghost proofing around the house."

I raise a brow. "You cleaned up the salt and iron filings around the windows and doors?"

Only in my house would that statement be said with a straight face.

"Most of the door salt had already worn away. The lack of a barrier is how Blake managed to appear a couple of months ago."

After he died, Blake had appeared to warn me about Agramon, the fear demon, and its diabolic plans. Which I managed to thwart. Once I killed Agramon, Blake returned to heaven, or wherever ghosts go when they aren't haunting humans. Bottom line, I haven't seen him since.

Which is just as well. He needs his happy ending and I need to get on with my life. A little hard to do if he continued to hang around.

Smythe ignores the reference to Blake while pointing out the obvious. "You haven't said what she wanted. Or her name."

T shakes off my palm and runs a hand across his super-short hair. "Her name is Lillian Feeley. She told an odd story about Eloise."

Smythe freezes for a second, his eyes widening almost imperceptibly. If I hadn't been looking at him, I wouldn't have caught the expression, it cleared his face so fast.

"What about Eloise?" His voice lowers, a hint of protectiveness in its depths.

"It's a strange story. You might want to sit?"

I do as my twin asks, plopping beside him on the couch. Smythe walks around so he faces us, arms crossed, stance wide, in full friend-defense mode.

T raises a brow at Smythe's stance before speaking. "She said Eloise was around when she was alive and Lillian died over seventy years ago."

"Healers age slowly. No surprise she's over seventy." Smythe states the fact in a dry tone indicating no big deal.

"Maybe not for you, but it surprised the shit out of me." My twin glares.

No wonder he was surprised at Eloise's age. He discovered his crush is a cougar.

"Go on." I pat his arm in encouragement, wanting to hear more about my newfound ghostly relative. So much for previously convincing myself not to learn more about my ancestors. When faced with an actual relative, I suddenly want to know all about my ancestry.

"As I was saying." T cuts a glance to Smythe. "She knew Eloise. When Lillian got pregnant and the mage father died before they married, she was freaked out. Not her words, but being a single mother wasn't the norm then. Since she was the sister of a *Justitian* and therefore next in line to wear the *justitia*, she had to follow the Agency's policies. Per policy, Lillian was required to register the pregnancy with the Agency, but Eloise convinced her otherwise. Eloise claimed there were demons in the Agency who wanted to take over and eliminate the *Justitians*."

"Demons?" Smythe slams his hands on his waist, a bunch of not-buying-it written across his face. "That's impossible. The Agency is warded against demon intrusion."

"Dude, I'm just telling you what she said."

Smythe walks around the coffee table and sits on the arm chair. "Go on."

After a slight head shake, T continues. "Eloise managed to convince Lillian the demon would kill her baby. So instead of registering her pregnancy, she took a vacation with Eloise, gave birth and gave the child, a girl, up for adoption. Several months later, Lillian was walking to the store when she was nailed by a car and killed."

"Why didn't Eloise heal her?" Eloise always was there for me. If she went to all the trouble to convince Lillian to give my grandmother up for adoption, wouldn't Eloise have been there for my great-grandmother?

"I got the impression Eloise didn't know about it until it was too late. She can't be in all places at once."

"What happened to the child, our grandmother?"

"Lillian said she watched her child, Donna, off and on from wherever ghosts stay. Donna never got along with her adoptive parents and left home as soon as she graduated from high school. She got knocked up and in her last month of pregnancy something went wrong and she died."

My eyes widen. "That's awful!"

"Yeah it is. Since Donna didn't leave the name of the father, or any family, our mother went up for adoption and we know the rest of the story."

"Tell her thanks for solving Gin's—and your—ancestry puzzle for me."

T nods at Smythe.

Smythe drums his fingers against his leg, eyes narrowed in thought. "Eloise was behind all this? She's known Gin's history all along?"

Red tinges T's cheeks at Smythe's questions. I'm sure he doesn't want to admit his crush appears to have an agenda of her own. I'm there with him. Eloise has saved me from death several times, which makes her one of the good guys, or gals as the case may be.

I don't want to think of her as knowing things about me and T and failing to mention them to us. Important things, like who our ancestors were, what made my *justitia* important, and why she thought a demon lived at the Agency.

I mean, I agree with her about the demon. Or demonic influence. Something was definitely wacky about my esteemed employer.

"I'm sure she had her reasons for keeping things from us." T's eyes narrow.

"Think you can find them out?" Smythe asks.

T crosses his arms. "Whatcha mean?"

"He means," I give T's arm another pat, trying to calm his defensiveness, "if you could ask her what she knows. She seems to like you and we know how you feel about her. We'll never know her reasons unless you ask."

T's glare lessens after a moment. "Okay. And what if you don't like what she says?"

"We might not like it, but at least we'll know. I'd rather know what happened in our family and why I can wear this bracelet"—I hold up my wrist, giving it a shake—"than never know the reasons. Wouldn't you?"

His lips press together as his jaw tenses. White lines form around his mouth then dissipate as his body relaxes. He nods. "Yeah, okay. I'll do it."

Chapter Fifteen

Under the guise of wanting to learn more about becoming a ghost-talker, T asks Eloise to come over right then. A bit of me feels duplicitous, as if I'm setting her up for a fall. Which I'm not. We're setting her up so we can learn the truth.

Eloise's brow furrows when she portals into my living room. Being blind doesn't mean she can't sense three people staring at her. And she's admitted to me she can see out of the eyes of people she is emotionally close to. Judging by her reaction, all of us must be in the close-friend category.

Excitement morphs to guilt. She's my friend. Perhaps this was a bad idea.

But before I can voice my hesitation, T speaks.

"Have a seat." T grabs her hand, leading her to the couch. Eloise turns her head toward Smythe and me before sitting next to my twin. "I asked you here about a ghost I talked to today."

"Is that the only reason?"

Good thing she can't see the blush stealing across T's cheeks. He clears his throat.

"The ghost I saw was my great-grandmother, Lillian Feeley. She said she knew you."

Eloise stills. "I see. What did she tell you?"

"You claimed the Agency had been infiltrated by demons and convinced her to give her child up for adoption."

Eloise sucks in her bottom lip, her gaze fixed halfway between T beside her and Smythe in the arm chair. After a long moment, she sighs. "Yes. I am guilty as charged. Is that what you wanted to know?"

"We'd like to know why," Smythe says. "You never mentioned any of this to me, even though you knew I was looking for Gin's ancestral history."

"I like you Aidan, but I couldn't be sure you wouldn't tell others. I need this to remain quiet."

"Why? Why would you hide Lillian, a potential *Justitian* who is the last of her line? Especially knowing we need all the help we can get."

Another long pause coupled with a furrowed brow and sucked in lips. She sighs. "If I tell you, will you swear to silence? It cannot leave this room."

What happens in Gin's house, stays in Gin's house.

We all swear to silence. Eloise nods. I lean forward. Maybe now I'll learn the answers to all my nagging questions.

"All right, then. I," she swallows, as if the words are distasteful, "I discovered a demonic presence in the Agency. It changes forms so I can feel it, but not identify it. It has been there for years, since shortly before the last *Justitian,* Lillian's sister, wore your bracelet, Gin. Anyway, I overheard the demon talking about its plans. About how it would kill your lineage and take the *justitia* for itself."

"How?" I ask. "Only a *Justitian* of its lineage can wear this bracelet. A demon wouldn't be able to wield it."

As soon as I spoke the words, I realized it wasn't entirely true. The bracelets were forged by the demons.

Perhaps the demons figured out a way to take their bracelets back.

Eloise confirms my thoughts. "Demons forged the bracelets. The original wearers, before they were called *Justitians*, discovered a spell to release them from their bondage. A spell that reversed the demons' control over them and allowed them to seek revenge upon those who enslaved them."

"What role did the Agency play?" The shocked expression on Smythe's face stands in opposition to his calm tone.

A half-grin turns her lips. "A group of mages learned of the females' plight and swore to help them defeat the demons. Millennia later, we have the Agency and *Justitians*. And the reason why you cannot create more bracelets. You never knew the original spell. No one did. Except for the demons."

"How do you know all this?" Especially since the Agency lost this history.

She smiles at my question, a grin telling me the secret is for her and her alone. Ignoring my question, she continues with the original story of my family history, the smile fading from her lips. "Unfortunately, my plan to save your lineage backfired. Your grandmother was adopted and I thought I had managed to prevent the line from dying. Then Lillian was killed—"

"She said it was an accident." T's brows furrow in confusion.

"It was made to look like one. But the Agency ordered it."

"Why?" The glare on Smythe's face could melt ice. "The Agency needs *Justitians*."

"Gin's bracelet controls the others. If the demon within the Agency can obtain her bracelet, then it will control the other *Justitians*."

What the hell? She can't be serious. A quick glance at Smythe shows he mirrors my surprise. "You mean I can control my fellow *Justitians*?

She shakes her head. "Not to my knowledge. Only the demons can use the *justitias* for that purpose since they are the creators."

Always nice to know I won't be tempted to be the "Head Bitch-In-Charge."

"Do you want to know this story, or do you want to continue to interrupt?" Her glare bounces between Smythe and me.

"Sorry." I'm not and neither is Smythe and she probably knows it, but she nods her head as if placated.

"As I was saying, the Agency put a hit on Lillian at the same time they sent her sister to kill Hitler. The sisters died within days of each other. I could not save either of them. I learned of their deaths too late. But I was comforted that Lillian's child was safe and the *justitia*—your *justitia,* Gin—was secured in the magical vault. I thought I could keep track of Donna and when she was grown, train her, and we could defeat the demon."

She lowers her eyes, her voice quieting. "But again, I was wrong. She left home and I lost track of her. I discovered she died so I thought all was lost. Then you appeared wearing the *justitia*. And I knew things would be all right."

"And you didn't think I should know this?" The low tone of Smythe's voice indicates his displeasure.

He's not the only one. I wish Eloise would have

mentioned my maternal history earlier.

"As I said, I couldn't risk you telling anyone else. I'm sorry if this offends." She pauses. "Did Lillian say anything about Donna having a child? I never found evidence of a child, and yet, Gin is able to wear the *justitia*."

T nods. "Yeah, she did. Donna gave birth to our mom but died due to pregnancy complications."

A pained look crosses Eloise's face. "How sad. I wish I had known. Perhaps I could have helped her. And your mother?"

"She lived until I was in college." The memory of coming home to find Mom dead on the couch, having drunk herself into oblivion one last time, never ceases to bring a lump to my throat.

"I'm sorry."

I nod while changing the topic to something on a happier note. Like one of my many unanswered questions. "Do you know what happened to my *justitia*? Like, how it disappeared from a magically secure vault?"

Eloise turns to me, a half-grin back on her lips. "It didn't disappear. I helped steal it."

Smythe's eyes pop wide. "You stole it? Why the hell would you help steal it?"

"Like I said, a demonic influence had woven through the Agency. Others were being turned to the dark side." One side of her lip twitches as she says, "dark side." "I knew what the demon wanted. I knew it wanted your *justitia*. And what better way to thwart a demon than to hide what it wants? Other mages knew what was happening and helped me out. I stole it, gave it to them and they hid it, keeping it safe."

"They died, you know." I glare at her, remembering Will's grief through our empathic connection, his fright as a minion murdered his mother.

Eloise nods as if their deaths were inconsequential. "They knew death was a possibility if they were discovered. They accepted this outcome to keep your bracelet safe. They died unsung heroes in order for you to wear the *justitia*. In order for you to fight and kill the Agency demon."

"You mean it's up to me to stop this demon you've been unable to stop for over seventy years?" What the hell? Was she smoking dope or something? How could I kill a demon this strong when I couldn't even win my fight with Rahab? When I almost gave in to Perdix?

"Don't sound so incredulous, Gin. You will fight and you will win."

At least someone thinks I can do this. I'm not so sure.

"I still can't believe you didn't trust me enough to tell me this." Smythe crosses his arms.

"I see now it was a mistake. I trust you Aidan. I wouldn't have told you this otherwise."

Smythe narrows his eyes. "Who's the demon? Who has it influenced at the Agency?"

His unspoken question floats on the air, unnoticed by T and Eloise. But I see it in the lines of his face, in the tightness of his lips, the tense of his jaw. Was his father involved?

"I don't know. I'm blind." One side of her lips kicks up. "Seriously, though. I can't tell. I know it's there. I can feel a demonic presence at the Agency. But I can't narrow down who it comes from. One day I'll feel a presence on a person, but the next I won't. I don't understand how it can hide so well. I should know who it is but every time I think on it, I get a headache and my mind skitters to another topic."

"Why didn't you do anything about this earlier?"

"Why do you think I hid Gin and T's grandmother? I tried. It wasn't enough."

"And there wasn't anyone you could trust?"

Her grin turns brittle. "Trust does not come easily for me. At the time, not many trusted me. Trust is earned and I had not earned it with the ones who counted. By the time I earned trust, the leadership changed and some of them seemed influenced by the demon so I could no longer trust them. At the time your *justitia* was stolen, others saw what I did. Those were the mages who helped me steal it."

"So now what?" My gaze pings between her and Smythe. "We know now what happened but what are we supposed to do about it? How do we ferret out the demon influencing the Agency? Does it still want my *justitia*? Does it have anything to do with the despair demon killing people here in Dallas?"

"So many questions." Eloise shakes her head. "I don't know. Yes, we need to stop the demon. Both demons. We'll probably have better luck with the one here than the one at the Agency."

"A double pronged approach." Smythe drums his fingers against his muscular thigh.

"What do you need me to do?" T asks.

We three look at him. From our expressions, we all think the same: how to tell him "nothing" without hurting his feelings.

Eloise breaks the silence. "I'm not sure. Unless you can talk to a ghost about who the demon is in the

Agency."

By the set of his jaw, ghost talking is not on his looking-forward-to-do list. His words, though, say nothing of his unease. "I can try."

Eloise nods. "I'll pick you up tomorrow."

"Guess I'm calling in sick." Instead of sounding excited, a hint of resignation threads through his voice.

"I vote Gin and I stop the despair demon while you two see what you can find out about the demon in the Agency." Smythe leans forward. "Sounds like it's been there for years. Perdix, on the other hand, is actively killing people. And will probably kill more. We'll hunt while you ferret out more clues about the Agency demon."

"Okay." A game plan. One that throws Smythe and me together. I take in his broad shoulders, the strong set of his jaw, the amount of willpower mixed with magic electrifying the air around him.

Weeks ago he lost his trust in me and now I can't give my trust to him. Okay, that's not true. I trust him to keep me safe. To help me fight demons. It's the trust in our romantic relationship I'm having a hard time piecing back together.

As if he feels the heat of my stare, his attention focuses on me. Heat smacks my cheeks as all sorts of not-appropriate-for-work thoughts zing through my brain. Did he send me a telepathic suggestion? Could he want me to participate in a little horizontal action? Do I want to?

Hell, yeah. Just not now. As shallow as it sounds, I'm not done with being mad at him. He hurt me. His actions were part of the reason I relapsed.

I drop my gaze to my lap.

Come on, Gin. Face the truth. You are responsible for your own actions. Passing the blame causes relapses and hurt feelings. My self-talk fails to help the trust issue.

Maybe one of these days.

"Dinner?"

T's voice pulls my head up. Everyone stares at me like I have the answer. Embarrassing. "What?"

"I said, did you want to have dinner?"

"You mean, did you want me to cook?"

"Same thing."

Twins. "Sure. Everyone staying?"

Everyone nods. Dinner it is.

Chapter Sixteen

My alarm wakes me by blaring in the darkness at 5:30 a.m. Why is it going off so early? Smythe isn't coming over until eight. I slap a hand on the off button, roll over, and continue snoozing.

A rap at my bedroom door wakes me. I mumble something, pull the covers over my head, and roll onto my side. The knock grows louder.

"Go away." The covers muffle my voice. Which clearly explains why the door opens.

"Why are you still in bed?"

What was Smythe doing here? He wasn't due until eight. I roll toward the door, lifting the covers enough to peek at the clock.

"Yikes!" I throw the covers off, heart pounding an "I'm late, I'm late" race.

Smythe leans against the door jamb, arms crossed, one brow raised as I stumble out of bed.

"Sorry." I rub my hands down my face, through my hair, trying to scrub away the tiredness as I talk. "My alarm went off at 5:30. I turned it off and went back to sleep without resetting it."

"Why did it go off at 5:30?"

I shrug. "Maybe it malfunctioned. It's not my day to—"

And then I remember. Work? My breath hitches. Oh my god, I'm supposed to be at work. At seven. It's now eight. What the hell was I thinking? How could I forget to show up for work?

Smythe's eyes widen as I go into full panic mode. "You were supposed to be at work today?"

"My phone." *Where did I leave my phone? Oh my god.* "I've gotta call in. She's going to fire me." No way will Nurse Hatchet keep me on staff if I don't show up and don't call in. How could I have forgotten about my job? My income? A shot of panic ricochets through my system, churning my stomach contents into a ball of writhing snakes.

I'm going to be fired.

My phone lies where I always put it, right by the alarm clock, but when I move to grasp it, my shaking hands knock it onto the floor instead. Damn it. Tears spring to my eyes. I'm so screwed. Smythe picks the thing up, unlocks it, brings up the phone app, and hands it to me.

Thank God he's around to help.

Panic rides me hard enough that the idea of him knowing my phone's PIN fails to faze me. Despite my trembling fingers, I manage to dial Ruth, a.k.a Nurse Hatchet. *Oh god, oh god, oh god. I don't want to be fired.*

My breath comes in short hitches as I blink away tears.

As soon as she picks up with a gruff "Hello," I start talking. More like gushing non-stop.

"It's Gin. I'm so sorry. My alarm didn't go off. I can be there in thirty." I hold my breath, as if it will help my ass not get canned.

A long pause ensues, during which the speedy, hard rhythm of my heartbeat echoes in my ears, a pounding of doom.

"Gin." Patience and concern lace her tone. The same tone I use when dealing with a difficult patient. It might hold concern, but doesn't bode well for my state of employment. "I've worked with you for years and you've always been a stellar employee. But lately, something has been off.

"You've missed work, you've been calling in excessively, you even had your brother call for you on Wednesday. I don't know what is going on with you but we can't have it. An emergency department cannot be staffed if personnel do not show up for work. Now, you are one of our best nurses and until recently have never had a problem. Because of your past work history, I'm willing to cut you some slack."

My breath comes out in a whoosh as I sag against the bed. "Thank you—"

"Don't thank me yet." Her tone hardens into inflexible resolve. Yep, I'm definitely screwed. "If you want to continue working here, you are going to need to go talk to a counselor. Either a psychiatrist or psychologist, I don't care which."

I gap at the phone for a second before putting it back against my ear.

"You mean at Blue Shores?" No way. I'd rather be fired than have another in-patient stint in a psychiatric hospital.

"Only if you want to. I have a friend in her own practice I could get you in to see. That is the condition to keep your job. And until she releases you, you will be on medical leave. If you don't accept these terms, you don't need to bother coming back to work. What do you say?"

See a shrink or be fired. Was there really a choice? The Agency won't pay me. Hell, the Agency might not even exist after we take down the demon haunting its esteemed halls. Provided we can kill the creature. Shrink it is. At least I'm not an in-patient this time.

The knowledge doesn't make me feel better. I'm so screwed. More like, I'm such a screw-up.

"Okay." My voice is small, tiny, scared.

Ruth says she'll call her friend then text me the name, number and time of my appointment, before she lets me go.

Right when my life seems like it is heading upward after taking a tumble into a deep grave, I fuck things up royally. My job as a nurse is my life. Or it was until the *justitia* found its way onto my wrist, until the entity in the bracelet wormed its way into my nervous system. What would I do without my nursing career? Without going into the Emergency Department? Without the rush of knowing I helped someone?

"What happened?"

Startled, I drop the phone onto the floor. Smythe is in my room? Lost in my own little pity party, I forgot he stands at the door, a concerned sentinel.

I sniff, my gaze focusing on the floor halfway between us. "She said if I see a shrink I can keep my job. She could set me up with a friend of hers, but if I don't talk to someone, then I can kiss my job good-bye." My voice cracks.

Dammit. I hate looking weak in front of Smythe.

I continue to look at the phone on the floor. Maybe if I crawl under the covers the day will start over.

Good luck with that wish.

"Did you agree to it?"

156

My gaze lands on his. "What do you think? Of course I agreed. I worked hard for my nursing degree and because of this *Justitian* gig I'm going to lose everything I accomplished. I can't let that happen."

He nods, hands raised in a placating gesture. "It'll be okay."

"No. It won't."

"What's going on in here?" T sticks his head in the door.

"I forgot I had to go in to work today." The words stick on my tongue, thick, heavy and full of failure.

T's eyes widen. "How can you forget your work schedule?"

"I don't know! My alarm sounded and I turned it off and wondered why I set it early. I've never missed a day until recently, which was my saving grace. Ruth didn't fire me, but she's making me see a shrink."

My phone beeps its text message sound. Right on cue. My appointment time.

I snatch the phone off the floor, unlock it and read the message. "The counselor's name is Kathy Funk. I'm supposed to be at her office this afternoon. 4PM sharp."

"We should be back from our hunt by then." Smythe pries the phone from my white-knuckled grip and places it on the nightstand.

Hunt? He still thinks I am capable of hunting a demon?

My expression must have given away my thoughts. Or I projected telepathically. Which I've been known to do on accident.

Yet another lack of capability.

Smythe and T give each other the quick glance men do when not sure what to say to a hysterical woman. I'm not hysterical though. Resigned maybe. Depressed, got it covered. Feeling like an utter moron? Yep. Most definitely. But hysterical? Nope. Not at all.

I sit on the bed. Before my legs shoved me into greater embarrassment by collapsing.

"You are a great demon hunter." Smythe bravely takes a step closer. "You killed two in the first couple of months wearing the *justitia*. That's a record."

"Yeah," T chimes in. "You do a bang-up job on those demons."

"Cut the bullshit. Just leave me alone guys, okay?"

Smythe runs his hand down my arm in a gesture meant to show support. In a rare instance, he opens his emotions, allows me to feel his sorrow, his incompetence at fixing my current emotion.

I grab his hand, bringing it to my lips for a quick kiss on his palm. While I appreciate his actions, I really don't want him in here with me. I want to grieve my potential job loss in silence.

"I'll go cook breakfast." He touches my cheek with the hand I'm not holding, a lover's touch, a touch I'd crave if not for my current stupid mistake.

I release his hand and he slips out of the room. T takes his place.

"Chin up, Gin. You've lived through worse."

"Thanks. You're so encouraging."

He sits beside me on the bed. Wraps his arms around me in a stiff hug. Stiff from my side. Nonetheless, the peace felt in his arms surrounds me, relaxing me infinitesimally. I put my head on his shoulder, returning his hug as my muscles relax.

"You can't let a little thing like a lack of a job get you down."

I snort. Right. Lack of a job means lack of money which translates, eventually, into lack of house.

"Don't laugh at me. We both worked hard to get where we're at, but there are always other jobs out there. And besides, you're needed to take down the evil Agency. If not you, then who?"

"You sound like a motivational kid's cartoon." But it did make me feel better. A smidgeon better, but it's something, right?

"You know I'm right." He pats my back, once, twice, three times. He pulls back, holding me by the upper arms as he looks me in my teary eyes. "Now, go get dressed. We have a demon to catch. Make that two demons."

A hug later and he pulls my bedroom door shut behind him. Maybe he's right. The ER is just a job. Never mind it's the only job I've held since graduating from college, the only work situation I've been in, it's only a job. There're plenty more out there. At least a dozen hospitals in or around Dallas. Plenty of openings.

I bury my face in my hands for an ugly cry.

I'm a screw up. Eloise might think I'm needed to help find the demon in the Agency and Smythe believes I can find Perdix. But I know better. Not only have I made mistakes as a *Justitian*, I completely spaced on my work schedule.

A wisp of warm air ruffles against me a second before the *justitia* forms a sword. Somehow it misses my head. I drop my hands at the same time a voice sounds. "I can get rid of your problems if you'll let me."

I release a gasp. Perdix leans against the doorjamb to the bathroom, arms crossed. In person. Not a projection. A demon stands in my bedroom.

I'm so shocked he's in person and not in my mind I sit frozen on the bed, tears dripping off my chin. Clearly this day can get worse.

"You wear his mark." I assume, by his bony finger pointing at my neck, the "his" refers to Zagan since it's Zagan's mark below my hairline. "I should kill you."

One thing in life you can always count on: a demon making death threats.

Before I can respond, he continues. "But, it is more fun to encourage you to capitulate to my thrall."

Whatever, demon. I might be a screw-up of epic proportions, but I have killed demons and know what to do with the pointy end of my sword.

I spring forward, slicing through the air, aiming for his neck, only to embed the *justitia* in the door frame as Perdix disappears.

Damn it. Wonder how much the repairs are going to cost?

"Tsk, tsk, tsk."

I twist at the sound behind me, unable to pull free to turn. The demon stands on the other side of my bed shaking his head.

Great. Now two demons are disappointed in me. How big of an idiot do you have to be for two demons to get upset with you?

I look back at the sword buried in the doorframe. Yeah, not answering that question.

Using my free hand to grasp my opposite forearm below the silver links of the *justitia*, I use the extra force to yank on my arm, hoping to free the sword from the wood.

"You don't have to be so violent about it."

Yank. The sword moves a wee bit.

"All you have to do is ask me to free you from this life."

Yank. Will the damn demon not shut up?

"Despite you belonging to my rival, I will happily welcome you into my arms."

Yank, yank, yank. Oomph. I land with a thud on my ass as the wood releases its hold on the sword.

"What grace. What poise. You are truly the most elegant servant Zagan has ever made."

I shove to my feet, pointing the sword at the smirking demon.

"Why did you kill all those people? I thought you fed on the dying, not those who still wanted to live."

"Power, my dear, power. Do you know how tasty a soul is when they don't want to die?" He smacks his lips. "Much better than the soul who dies by despair alone. Despair mixed with fear is quite the energy giver." He smacks his lips again.

"And what, you absorb all this energy to be able to stalk more victims?" I take a step backward toward the door as I speak, stopping when the knob touches my backside.

A small smile curves his lips. "Not victims, my dear; hasn't your master explained this to you?"

"He's not my master." I reach behind, twist the knob, and step forward, opening the door. "Smythe!"

During the brief time my head turns to yell at my mentor, the demon pulls a vanishing act, leaving with the same wisp of warm air on which he arrived.

My sword still points at the empty space on the other side of my unmade bed when Smythe, T, and Eloise run into the room.

"What?" Smythe puts a hand on my shoulder, his touch radiating heat.

The *justitia* morphs into a bracelet with a tiny *snap*, drawing everyone's attention to my wrist.

"Perdix popped in for a visit." I wave my hand at the demon's last known location.

Smythe raises a brow. "Popped in? As in he was here and not invading your mind?"

"Yep. In person."

Anger radiates off T as he fights to keep his "your job is dangerous and you need to quit it" thoughts to himself. So much for him thinking me necessary to fight demons.

"Why didn't you kill him?"

I rub the back of my neck and sniff as heat splashes my cheeks. "He was standing by the bathroom and I swung, he disappeared, and the sword caught in the frame."

Smythe walks over to the frame, his shoulders shaking as if he's laughing at me. Okay, no "as if" about it. My mentor was laughing at my expense.

But when he turned around, all the mirth was gone. "Let's go."

He's halfway through his portal forming words before the shock wears away, freeing my thoughts.

"Go? I'm not dressed."

Once he opens the portal, his gaze draws down my body and back up, leaving behind a wash of warmth. "We need to make sure the demon hasn't returned to his lair. Come on."

What is it about Smythe yanking me through portals when I'm dressed for bed? I wore this same outfit when we first met and he took me to the Agency.

Good way to meet my new employer.

Lesson learned: stop sleeping in boy shorts and a tank top.

"Do you need us?" T asks, his voice a low growl. He gestures between him and Eloise.

Smythe shakes his head while grabbing my hand. "We'll be back. The house is in this neighborhood."

Not waiting for a response, he pulls me in my skimpy sleeping clothes into the portal. This is definitely the last time I'm wearing this attire to bed.

Chapter Seventeen

We land on the side of the same demon-infested house we explored yesterday. Since my *justitia* remains in bracelet form, I assume the demon picked another place to haunt.

"It's chilly, can we go home?" I raise my wrist, give the bracelet a shake to show Smythe it wasn't a sword.

Brows furrowed, he stares at me as if I spoke in some weird language. "Chilly? It's sixty."

"Sixty is chilly for Texas and this outfit." I gesture to my goosebumped legs under my boy shorts. "You should've let me change. How am I supposed to fight a demon looking like this?"

Smythe pauses, giving me another down-up raking gaze, setting off another round of goosebumps having nothing to do with the temperature and everything to do with heat of a whole different kind. "Come on. We'll check the demon trails from inside the house so you can warm up."

The missing-a-hinge gate to the backyard offers him no pause as he shoves the squeaky thing open, striding into the weed-covered yard as if he owns the place. Grass brushes against my legs as I follow. Hopefully everyone is already at work and won't notice me hurrying through the yard in my sleep clothes.

When we get to the backdoor, Smythe pauses,

"ready for action" written in his cocked-brow expression. I nod. Might as well get this over with.

He shoves open the door, palm facing forward, ready to throw a spell if needed. Since my *justitia* remains in bracelet form, his readiness probably wasn't needed. Unless of course Perdix pops into the room through a portal.

I follow behind my mentor, searching the corners for fresh trails or any other evidence of a recent demon presence while ignoring the touch of cold creeping down my spine.

Nothing pops out to scare me.

Except for my reflection in the bathroom mirror. Yikes. Instead of worrying about my skimpy outfit, I should've been worrying about a grade A case of bed-head.

Running a hand through my hair, I trail Smythe into the master bedroom.

"He's not here." My mentor looks like someone stole his favorite toy.

"The demonic trails are almost faded too. Looks like he hasn't used this place for several days."

Smythe's eyes narrow. "The Agency computer should've reported his appearance."

"The thing is off more than it's on. They need to replace it."

"They think it works fine."

Further proof something fishy is going on at the Agency. How can they not realize the demon-finding program is faulty? Unless…

"Maybe someone tampered with it. After talking to Eloise we both know it could happen. If there's a demon in the Agency, and I've been saying all along

165

something odd is going on there, then maybe the demon tinkered with the program. Made it so the thing doesn't always report a demon appearance."

Smythe stares at me for a moment before rubbing the bridge of his nose. "I can't believe a demon hides in the Agency and no one has caught on. Eloise is talking about a demon being there for over seventy years. Seventy years. Surely someone would've caught the thing by now."

"It sounds wily and good at hiding. Rather like Perdix is turning out to be. Where do you think he went?"

The Agency demon has been around for years. Perdix is killing people in my city. He's going down first.

"Another house? He could be anywhere since he visited in person." Smythe gestures around the room. "I thought he'd be here now."

"It was a good thought. Here's another one. Let's go back, change clothes—well, I'll change, you look fine—eat breakfast and then we can try to chase this demon. After I've had my coffee."

Ah-ha. No wonder I couldn't think of a place the demon could be. I was running on empty and needed a large dose of caffeine.

Smythe pauses, giving me his "you're such an addict" look. "Okay. Deal. Then we'll hunt until your appointment."

My whole body stiffens at the thought of going to the counselor, an involuntary flinch my ever-watchful mentor notices.

"No need to worry. She'll ask you questions. You'll answer. No problem."

He doesn't understand.

"What don't I understand?"

Geesh, not again. "You think you can teach me how not to project my thoughts?"

"We've been through that lesson." His lips twitch.

"I need a touch up."

"Try telling me what I don't understand."

Goosebumps prickle my flesh as my words escape in a rush. "I don't like shrinks, okay? Bad experience. Can we go home now?"

"Tell me about it." A trace of compulsion laces his words, but I manage to shake it off.

"Not now."

He crosses his arms. "I can't help you if you don't tell me."

I swallow, glancing at the dirty carpet. The fibers hold no answers, only grime. What harm would it do to tell him? Would he think different of me if I told the whole truth? He might. Although he deserves to know.

Little white lies, Gin, little white lies.

"I was sent to a psychiatric ward when I was a teenager. It wasn't pleasant and I don't want to repeat the experience. Any part of the experience." A shiver cascades through my limbs as memories threaten an appearance.

"Because you're an empath?"

"You mean, were my empathic abilities the reason I was sent?" He nods at my question. I draw in a breath. "Yeah, something like that."

I pause, my memory tripping backward in time. "After my father d"—oops, not mentioning the "dead" word. To cover, I clear my throat—"disappeared, I had a, um, breakdown," more like got high at school and went nuts, but who wants to admit major screw-ups? "At school. I was raving about how I could see everyone's thoughts.

"Which didn't go over well and long story short, I wound up at a psychiatric unit for troubled teens. I wasn't there long. Once I stopped saying out loud what others were feeling when I touched them, they let me go." I offer him a half-grin. "I'm a quick study. Can we go home now? I'm cold."

Cold permeates my soul, shaking my insides. Not the chill from the outside air—no matter what Smythe thinks sixty degrees in Texas is cold—but the chill that comes from opening up to someone, from baring my past.

His hand on my shoulder jerks my gaze to his. Fingers stroke with a feather-light touch down to my wrist where he grabs my palm, offering me a squeeze of support.

"I'm sorry. It must've been hard for you."

He has no idea. To convince a trained professional nothing was wrong, that I hadn't gone tripping to cover murdering my father—or as I called it at the time, liberating us from his abuse—or had any empathic tendencies took some effort in the form of lies and redirection.

I've been caught in those lies and redirection ever since.

None of which I mention. "Yeah. It was. Enough sharing. Really, I want out of these clothes."

Giving my palm another squeeze, Smythe releases me, holding his hand in front of him while speaking his portal forming words.

A few seconds later we're back in my bedroom.

Smythe leaves me alone, pulling the door shut behind him. Voices sound from the kitchen, muffled through the wall, but enough to let me know he's telling T and Eloise about our lack of finding Perdix.

Yet another thing I fail at, finding demons.

I give myself a mental smack. *Snap out of it, Gin.* Until recently, depression had never been on my playlist. The sooner we put down the damn despair demon, the better I'll be.

Maybe eliminating Perdix won't absolve me of my mistakes. Only I possess the ability to forgive myself for killing Donny. And I'm not yet sure I'm ready to stop punishing myself for his death.

I run a hand through my bed-head as I head toward the dresser for a bra and panties. Perhaps seeing the counselor this afternoon is for the best. All these thoughts of Perdix, Donny, and depression running through my mind on a continuous loop can't be good for me.

On the flip side, I can't tell the shrink any of my demon huntress experiences. Mentioning anything about demons or killing Donny will put me in the loony bin. If the would-be killer hadn't been blamed for Donny's death, I'd face jail time for admitting to killing the football star. Even if I admitted it, the counselor might decide I was half-crazy and have me committed to Blue Shores psychiatric hospital.

Which means I should come up with something plausible for the counselor as to why I've been missing work.

Good thing I'm skilled at lying my ass off.

Chapter Eighteen

A shower and some clean clothes later, I step into my bedroom dressed and ready to meet the day. A glance in the mirror shows determination plastering my face into a semi-normal expression. A gnawing ache sets up residence in my stomach, unease and revulsion fighting for dominance. Why, oh why, did I forget my work schedule? *What an idiot.*

Stop it Gin. Those thoughts can only lead to another visit by Perdix.

I'd rather spill my guts to the shrink.

My phone starts ringing the moment I reach for the bedroom doorknob. The number for Blue Forest Emergency flashes on the screen. Why is work calling after telling me to stay home?

"Hello?"

"Gin? It's Will. Why aren't you at work?"

I draw in a deep breath. Since when does Will call me? Didn't Smythe give him his number to call? Could he be calling about starting his mage training lessons?

"Long story. Whatcha need?" Because he clearly needs something. He might be my friend, but he hasn't called me in over fourteen years since we went to high school together.

He lowers his voice to a whisper. "Have you caught the demon yet?"

"Not yet. Working on it. Why?"

He pauses, the sound of his fingers tapping against a hard surface echoes through the phone. *Tap, tap, tap.* "If you haven't caught it, I want to help you do so. He killed my dad, the man who practically raised me. And a minion killed my mom and probably my birth dad too, so I owe the bastards some payback."

Yep, I was right. Will is confirming his decision to become a mage. I should be happy he wants to embrace his heritage. Instead, my first thought is to protect him from the demon-killing life.

"And how exactly do you plan on doling out revenge? You have to learn spells, you can't just go in half-cocked and expect to win against a denizen of hell."

"You do."

My chuckle sounds evil. "Right." I draw out the word. "I come equipped with a fancy demon-fighting sword. And I never go in half-cocked." Which is a lie, but hey, I have a point to make and don't want him to get hurt.

"The guy you hang out with, what's his name?"

Sure, Will forgot. How can anyone forget Smythe? "Aidan Smythe."

"Yeah, him. Anyway, he said he'd call to set up my training lessons but I haven't heard from him. I'm ready to fight. The least he can do is call."

"Can you hang on a minute?"

"Why?"

"Just wait." I stick the call on mute, open the bedroom door and yell for Smythe.

Who comes running like the place is on fire and I'm the only one with a fire extinguisher.

"What?"

I wave the phone. "Will's on mute. He says you never called him to set up training lessons and he wants to help us take down this demon. What do you want me to tell him?"

Blue eyes blink in surprise. He holds out a hand and I put the phone in it. After unmuting the line, he hits the speaker button.

"Will, this is Aidan Smythe. Gin says you have questions?"

Will pauses. Despite him being miles away, I know the thought flowing through his mind: Smythe and Gin are together?

Hate to tell him the answer is currently nope.

Lucky for me, he keeps his "are they or aren't they" thought to himself. "Yeah, man, you never called me back. I'm willing to help take this thing down. Do you want my help or not?"

"Of course we want your help." Assurance fills Smythe's tone. "These things take time. I haven't heard back from my superiors about the training. But if you want to stop by Gin's tonight, I'll teach you some spells."

"What time? I don't get off work until around four this afternoon."

Smythe raises a brow at me. I nod. Why not let Will come over? I'll be at the shrink. A thought continuing to give me a case of nausea.

"That'll work." Smythe nods. "You know where she lives?"

"Nope. What's her address?"

I give it to him along with directions. In case his GPS breaks.

"Thanks. See you then." Will hangs up without

waiting for us to say "bye."

Smythe hands me my phone. "He can't go hunting with us."

"Duh. I know that. I don't want him hurt anymore than you do. But I am glad you're going to train him." A thought pops into my brain. I give him a saucy smile. "While you're at it, maybe you can teach me the compulsion spell? Not only how to fight it, but also how to use it." I raise my brows twice, pasting a smile on my lips.

He rolls his eyes. Shakes his head. "It's a hard spell to master. You have to work up to it. You aren't anywhere close."

Dammit. So much for compelling others to do what I say.

He pats my shoulder, eyes full of mirth. "Sorry. Breakfast is ready. We can plot our day."

"Thought it already was plotted." I grin, giving him a playful whack on the arm. "But I can always use the coffee. Not to mention your bacon and eggs are to die for."

He follows me into the kitchen where we heap food on our plates, grab coffee—me in my extra-large mug and him in a normal sized, a.k.a tiny, cup—and join T and Eloise at the table. The kitchen feels cramped, but in a good way. Friends getting together and bonding type of way. Friends who plot demon killings and takedowns together make a house feel homey.

Who knew?

"I'll take T to the Agency after we finish eating and see if there are any ghosts he can talk to," Eloise says.

"How are you going to get him past the guards?"

I'm assuming Smythe means the teenagers manning the computer stations in the white landing room. His opinion of their skills ranks higher than mine.

Hardness tints her grin. "Who said anything about guards?"

"The only way in—"

"Come on, Smythe," I point a piece of bacon at my guardian mentor. "You know well enough she pops into the infirmary without going through the landing room. Hell, she portals in and out of the Agency rooms at will, despite wards prohibiting portal forming anywhere in the building except the landing room. You really think she can't sneak T inside?"

Smythe glares. Not my fault he can't handle the truth.

T looks at the two of them, what-the-hell furrows lining his forehead. "The Agency is that well guarded? What difference does it make if a human gets in?"

"Secrets, my dear brother. The place crawls in secrets." I swear hidden machinations line the walls of the Agency like macabre paintings.

Smythe huffs. "The less humans know about demons, minions, and mages the better. It's for protection."

"You say protection, I say it's a great way to hide secrets from the masses." I nod.

"Either way, it still doesn't explain how she"— Smythe gestures to Eloise—"manages to get inside without going through the landing room. Care to explain?"

"Not really." Eloise takes a bite of egg.

T presses his lips together, eyes crinkling with

suppressed humor.

"Eloise."

"Aidan."

Smythe stares at her for a two count. The turn of her lips indicates that despite her blindness, she knows exactly his expression her lack of an answer provokes.

"If we are going to do this, if we are going to go on a witch hunt—"

"It's not a witch hunt, Aidan, it's a demon."

His eyes narrow. "It's an expression, Eloise. As I was saying, if we are going to go on a…demon hunt, then we need to know each others' skills. You already know mine. I thought I knew yours. Trust is mutual."

Eloise's red eyes blaze. "Suffice it to say the wards surrounding the Agency aren't strong enough to stop me. Any of them. If I want to enter, I can. From any location. Same with leaving. As far as trust, you have more reason to trust me than not to trust me. Unless you believe something changed?"

"Not with me."

"Good. Then it's settled. I'll take T to the Agency, let him look around, see if the ghosts are the kind who talk. You take Gin and try to stop this demon. Oh, speaking of Perdix, you never did tell us what he said to you this morning, Gin. Why did he appear in the flesh?"

I glance at my plate and swallow. "He came for me again." His visit gives me a topic to speak on besides my idiocy and shame.

"Perdix wants me because he thinks I'm Zagan's servant. Apparently the servant thing makes me a hot commodity on the demon market. I asked him about the recent suicide victims and why he was killing them as opposed to waiting until they wanted to die. He said it was a power trip but disappeared before I could ask him what he meant. Oh, he also said something along the lines of 'My master should have explained this.' I'm not sure what 'this' is. Are you?"

Eloise and Smythe exchange a look. I glance at T, who shrugs. A closer glance shows his jaw tensing and relaxing, tensing and relaxing. A light brush against his mind offers insight. *Fucking demon trash* plays over and over again. Which is an opinion he usually has no problem expressing.

Except when Eloise is around. Apparently he wants to hide his temper from her. My brother, in love with the healer. He might have the hots for Eloise, but no way could he completely be healed from Jackie's untimely death.

All questions for later.

Smythe clears his throat. "We're not certain what he means."

"Perhaps he is referring to things going on at the Agency."

I shake my head at Eloise's comment. "Why would he refer to the Agency as my master? I thought he was talking about Zagan. I'm just not sure what topic he thought Zagan was supposed to tell me."

"Why don't you ask Zagan?" Eloise asks.

I shrug, hoping the movement masks the hollow pit of loss from my current rocky relationship with the demon. "He's not speaking to me right now."

"We'll figure it out." Smythe raps his knuckles on the table. "Ready to hunt some evil?"

Chapter Nineteen

I slam my car door while staring at the five-story medical building next door to my hospital's campus. Demon hunting with Smythe was a bust. Despite canvassing my neighborhood for an hour, no demon or minion tracks were found except the faded ones at the abandoned, for-sale house. While happy to note I live in a demon/minion-free area, I'm not so happy to still have Perdix running around up to no good.

We also tried another round of interviews with family members of the deceased suicides. The few we caught at home all said the same thing: their loved one was not depressed. The victims were all upset over a recent occurrence, but not depressed with suicidal thoughts. None of the deceased wrote *Get away from me Satan* on loose pieces of paper like Will's foster dad, but most of them did rant about voices in their heads shortly before their deaths.

Freakin' demons.

And since this particular demon haunted me too, I held a personal grudge to kill its ass. Preferably sooner rather than later. Then I could get on with hunting the demon Eloise claimed lived at the Agency. Or getting my job back.

Which brings me to this office building where I'll need to tell a compelling lie about why I've been late and missing work. At least the lack of finding a demon meant I made my afternoon appointment on time.

Oh joy.

Okay, Gin, you got this. How hard could it be to lie to the good counselor, convince her I'm stable and get back to my house by dinner?

I draw in a deep breath. I'm screwed.

Positive thoughts, Gin, positive thoughts. I managed to get out of a psychiatric ward by lying. A feat much harder than lying to a counselor. I hope.

Maybe I'm not as screwed as I thought.

Striding across the parking lot, I pull my raincoat closer around my body. A fine mist floats in the air, wets my face. Dampness highlights the scent of oil staining the asphalt. The double doors of the medical office building slide open, admitting me to a marble-coated entry. Great flooring choice for ailing patients coupled with rain. Shaking my head, I shuffle my feet on the damp mat, trying to dry my shoes to avoid slipping on the slick marble tiles.

The elevator drops me off on the fourth floor. A quick peek at the signs on the wall directs me to the office. When I arrive in the waiting room, the receptionist hands me the obligatory paperwork to fill out. I take a seat on one of the overstuffed sofas lining the walls. Instead of winding me up tighter than I already am, the room relaxes me, soothing away my stress.

Clearly the counselor discovered a way to waft Prozac through the air vents.

Paperwork completed and returned to the receptionist, I sit on the sofa, flipping through a magazine. Five minutes past the hour, the door to what I assume to be the spill-your-guts office opens. An average build, brown haired, thirty-something man steps out, heading toward the smiling receptionist. A tall woman with short gray hair, a long flowing skirt and enough turquoise jewelry around her neck and ears to give the average person a trip to the chiropractor, stands in the doorway. Her smile welcomes me, draws me in, begs me to confide my deepest secrets.

My gaze can't leave hers. I want to tell her my problems, my real problems, not the fake ones I decided on while driving here.

"Gin?"

I stand, hold out my hand. "That's me."

"I'm Kathy Funk. You can call me Kathy."

She takes my hand when I reach the doorway, giving it a brief squeeze before stepping back to usher me into her private domain. The door clicks closed, but before I can sit, the main office door slams open, startling us.

"You fucking bastard, I knew I'd find you here! I told you I'm the only thing you need!" A woman's screech snaps my spine erect.

Kathy's eyes widen as if she's not used to having her office interrupted by an irate woman. A shifting of silver links on my wrist clues me in it's no irate woman. Double dog damn it. A minion screeches in the waiting room and a two-foot long sword juts from my wrist.

As Kathy pulls the door open, I make the obvious choice when faced with a soon-to-be-dead minion and a need for memory tinkering: call for help.

Smythe! There's a minion in the waiting room at my counselor's. Help! Come quick!

A pause and then his essence explodes into my mind, excitement coupled with a let's-get-this-done emotion guaranteed to put me in a fighting state of mind.

Coming.

As soon as Kathy steps into the waiting room, Smythe portals beside me.

Before I can ask him how the hell I'm supposed to kill a demon without anyone calling the cops or the men in white suits, the noise escalates. The male client yells at the minion—about her being a crazy-ass bitch—while Kathy tries to deescalate the situation using a soothing voice that would calm a normal human, but eases the minion about as much as slicing a hole in her stomach.

Smythe gestures at the door. "The cleanup crew can erase their memories. Go kill the damn minion."

Oh, yeah, right. I knew that. My panic moment kept my brain cells from firing.

I dart out the door into a scene from hell. Not really, but it sure did resemble one. Long minion fingers wrapped around the man's throat while he did his best to pull her off without making a direct hit. Kathy and the receptionist had joined in the tug-fest, trying to peel the minion's fingers from the man's throat. All three humans were getting nowhere fast. Blotchy spots colored the man's face an ugly shade of red.

"Step back!" I yank the receptionist free of the melee, shoving her to the side as I draw back my sword.

Kathy's eyes pop wide, but she moves out of the way of the impending blow. Unfortunately, so does the minion.

The man drops to the floor, hands around his bruised neck, as the minion leaps backward, avoiding my attempted slice.

"Bitch! Do you know who I am?"

Why is it demons and minions possess an inflated self-identity? I don't give a shit who she thinks she is. All I care about is she's a minion, which means she must die. End of story.

Drawing my sword up at the ready, I step toward her. "I don't care."

Evil creeps through her smile. "I belong to Rahab."

Oh, goody. One of Rahab's wanna-be's. I might be unable to kill the demon, but I can take down all his ego-inflated minions.

Spit bubbles in the corners of her mouth as she screams her qualifications, obviously assuming they would impress me to the point of giving up. Fat chance, minion.

"I'm the best there is. The best. I'm the best girlfriend ever in the history of the world. But that fool," she points to the man, "left me for some bitch not nearly as good as me. He deserves to die. Get out of my way, *Justitian*."

She runs at me. I swing. Not fast enough, though. Red oozes from the slice on her arm. A gasp comes from one of the three humans who watch our fight. The minion rubs her hand over her bleeding upper arm, a snarl twisting her face into pure evil.

"That hurt, bitch."

"So sorry I missed."

She circles around, me mirroring her movements, a dance to the death.

She young. Easy to kill. Let me in. The *justitia's* voice echoes in my head. *I end her now. No play.*

Alrighty then. If the entity along my nerves wants

to kill the minion, so be it.

I draw in a deep breath, eyes focused on the minion who stares at me, both of us watching the other for the smallest movement. Purple light flares, obscuring my vision for a split second, a clear indication the *justitia* powers my movements. My body moves faster than I thought possible.

While the *justitia* has taken control of my limbs before in a fight, it's been nothing like this speed. A heady power rush fires off a sense of euphoria. Whatever changed between the entity and me, I like it.

My body moves in a blur of speed not even the minion with her hyper-acute senses can track. One minute she stands snarling at me, eyes scanning my body for a subtle twitch indicating an impending attack, and the next blood spurts across the blue and white sofas as her head drops to the floor with a rolling thud.

The sound of her head and body hitting the white carpet echoes in my mind, a slow-motion reel of horror. My body slows to normal, no longer the super-fast speed used to kill the minion.

Screams and gasps reverberate against blood spattered walls, background noise barely registering as I use the flat of my blade to catch the demon's essence before it escapes back to its host. The gray mist sizzles on my *justitia*, destroying a small part of the demon. Kill enough of a demon's minions and you'll kill the demon. Eventually.

I turn. The man sits on the ground, the receptionist kneeling beside him, both staring at me, faces frozen in horror. Kathy takes a step back, eyes wide. I glance down at my blood-spattered clothes. Crap. There went another outfit.

When I raise my eyes, Smythe stands in the doorway to Kathy's private office, holding up a finger, phone against his ear. In the silence I hear the words, "cleanup crew STAT." Good to know they're on their way. Even better to know he had enough confidence in my minion fighting abilities to stay out of the way and let me handle it.

Maybe I'm not as big of a screw-up as I thought.

Harsh breathing dominates the small space. I should say something, should try to ease their fears, but what difference did it make? Soon the cleanup crew would erase their memories, leaving them with some happy-happy the formerly soothing office could never hope to match.

I look at Smythe as the three continue to bounce gazes from the headless minion to my no-longer-a-sword *justitia.*

I thought you were going to help. Telepathy rocks. Especially in a situation where humans—even if they are about to have their memories erased—don't need to know when you're questioning your boss's judgment.

Didn't need to. You had it covered.

And don't those words give a girl a case of the smiles. He thinks I'm a good fighter. A far cry from when we first started. Also nice to know he didn't abandon me like last time.

I offer him a grin.

When we get back, you'll need to tell me what you did to move so fast. You blurred out. I had trouble following you.

Before I can respond, the man recovers enough to speak, pointing at the headless minion as he clears his throat, his raspy voice an indication of a throat injury.

"What the hell was the gray mist that came out of her?"

I glance at Smythe, who shakes his head. I look back at the man's wide-eyed expression. What difference does it make if he knows? Whatever I tell him will disappear soon enough. Ignoring Smythe's continued head shaking, I answer. "Demon essence."

Amazingly enough, human eyes can widen to cover half a face. "Seriously? Like she was possessed?"

"Yep." I nod.

He turns to a pale-faced Kathy. "See? I told you she was the devil's bitch."

Kathy continues to stare at the minion, green tingeing the counselor's pale face as her gaze bounces to the streaks of blood turning her calming office into a macabre crime scene. Ignoring her client, she turns to me, her head tilting. "You killed her."

"She was a minion." My eyes narrow. "A demon's minion. She deserved to die. Her kind wreak havoc on earth."

"But you killed her." Her soft tone holds…wonder?

Smythe steps into her office, disappearing from view, the movement snagging my gaze. Low voices escape. The cleanup crew has arrived.

As I return my gaze to Kathy, a memory plays in my mind, a reminder of how naïve I was several months ago. When I first started this demon-killing gig, I thought minions could be saved. If only I could convince them of the demon's evil, convince them to forsake the bad for the good, I could draw out the demonic essence, returning them to human status.

It never happened. It never will happen. Maybe if I catch a person before they decide to become a minion, before demon essence enters their body, corrupting their soul, then I can save them. Like I tried to do with Donny.

Maybe I should forgive myself for killing the football star. He would've swallowed Rahab's evil essence whole, without a second thought. Donny showed no remorse for cozying up to a demon; why should I feel bad for killing him before he hurt a lot of people?

Epiphanies one has in a shrink's office.

Oh, yeah, I might want to answer said shrink before the cleanup crew erases her memory. It might not matter in the grand scheme of things, but for whatever reason, I want her to understand.

"She couldn't be saved. She was no longer a woman, she was a minion. You can't save minions. You can only kill them before they kill you."

Her eyes focus on me. "That's what you do isn't it? Kill these," she waves a hand at the body, "things. That's why you've been missing work."

I blink at her insight as Smythe steps out of the office, two mages behind him, obliterating my chance for an answer.

"Nice kill," one of the mages says, nodding his head as he looks at the body.

Kathy turns as she glares at the three mages, red splotches obliterating the paleness of her face. "Who the hell are you and what are you doing in my office?" She steps forward, hands planted on her hips, confusion and anger replacing her fear.

The two mages stop, eyes widening before they squeeze them shut and shake their heads. Almost as if she threw a spell at them. Which I'm pretty sure she didn't, judging from her red face and trembling hands. Not to mention she's a counselor, not a mage. Diagnosis: adrenaline rush after danger. Clearly the mages were surprised by her temerity.

"Ma'am," one of the mages places a hand on her shoulder. "All you saw was an argument. All any of you saw was an irate woman—"

"But she's my ex-girlfriend," the man interrupts the attempted spell. "I knew she was crazy. Like evil demon crazy. No one believed me."

The mage drops his hand from Kathy's shoulder, walks to the man, puts his hand on the guy's shoulder and looks into his eyes. "You are correct. She was crazy. She came in here irate, yelled at you, but then left when threatened with the police. Isn't that right?"

Three sets of eyes glaze as the mage writes a new story for what they saw. A shame he can't leave Kathy with the knowledge she deduced so she can understand why I miss work, so I don't have to lie to her. I've only just met her, but something about the woman makes me want to tell her the truth. About everything. And have her remember.

On the other hand, perhaps it's best her mind gets erased. Then I can stick to my tried and true lies with all my secrets intact.

While the mage continues his tale of the crazy woman yelling then leaving and what everyone saw and did, the other mage begins the process of magically scrubbing the room clean of blood. I look at my blood-stained clothes. Back to the clean walls.

It never hurts to ask.

"Hey," the room-cleaning mage turns as I approach. "Think you can get rid of this blood?" I gesture to my clothes. "I have an appointment with Kathy here and I'm sure she'll think I'm major nuts if I walk in looking like this."

The mage raises a brow. "An appointment?"

"It's a long story."

He shrugs, waves a hand and poof, my outfit is saved. I grin.

"Thanks, man."

He shrugs again, returning to his work.

I slide around both mages to Smythe.

"Think he can weave a tale about how I'm normal so I don't have to come back?"

Smythe cracks a smile, his eyes twinkling. "Making you normal would be too big of a stretch."

"Gee, thanks."

"Seriously, though. Would she really release you after one session?"

Sure, sits on the tip of my tongue, but I stop to think about it. Would she? The last trip to the shrink got me a week's stay in a psych ward before I convinced the good doctor to release me and Hell week included twice-daily counseling sessions. I sigh.

"Probably not."

He slaps a hand on my shoulder. "As much as I agree with you about these sessions, if you want to keep your job, you should suck it up and act like no minion interrupted your chat."

Normally I'd interject a bit about how the Agency should man up and pay for my salary so I can quit and work for them full time, but with all Eloise said about the place, I'm no longer so sure I want them to pay me. Was it dirty money if a demon had had his or her hands on it? Until we get the Agency demon killed, I'm better off with my nurse's salary.

Besides, I love being a nurse.

Which means I get to stay for a counseling session once this whole mess gets scrubbed clean.

Chapter Twenty

Smythe leaves to meet Will while the mages
continue to scrub the scene. Despite a dead body in the
waiting room, the mages manage to convince the man
and receptionist nothing strange occurred. Not sure
what memories they planted in the man's mind to
explain the time lapse, but as soon as he walked out the
door, they sat me in Kathy's office and told her we'd
had a successful hour session.

Once the mages give everyone shiny, new
memories, they disappear with the minion's body to rig
a crime scene not involving Kathy's male client. Nice
of them to divert blame from the poor guy. His bad
choice in women shouldn't result in being blamed for a
murder he didn't commit. As soon as they portal away
with the minion, Kathy snaps out of her trance. Right
on cue.

Her eyes squint as she presses fingers against her
forehead.

"Are you okay?"

She nods. "All of a sudden, I have a raging
headache."

"I'm sorry. I hope it feels better."

She stands, offering me her hand. "It will. As soon
as I pop some ibuprofen. Stop by the receptionist on the
way out and set up an appointment next week."

"Thank you."

I shake her hand. Her confusion and pain slip into my mind before our palms slide apart. She closes the door as soon as I step into the waiting room. Did all people with scrubbed minion memories have a headache? The receptionist didn't seem to be in pain. Neither did the male client before he left. Perhaps different people reacted differently to having mages invade their mind.

The waiting room once again relaxes me, all traces of the minion fight vanished from the mages' nifty room-scrubbing magic. I make an appointment for next week and hope the visit won't be as exciting.

While winning a minion fight is a good ego booster, I'd rather focus on the counseling session, i.e. getting my job back. Kathy seemed nice, which made the idea of spilling my lies harder than I feared.

When I arrive home, a Tesla sits in front of my house. A Tesla? Oh, right, Will was supposed to drop by for a mage training session with Smythe. A stab of jealousy sneaks in. I would love one of those cars. Unfortunately, the chances of me ever being able to afford it rank under the not-happening category.

Maybe he'll let me pet, I mean, touch it.

After opening the garage door, I drive inside, parking under the hanging sign telling me to "stop here." Once the garage door slides shut, I walk up the steps to the back porch, and open the kitchen door. Everything looks to be in place, no loud noises, no blown-up furniture or appliances, no evidence of dueling mages. Voices sound from the other room, hushed and barely discernible.

I place my purse on the counter then head to the living room. Will and Smythe sit facing each other on the couch. Will wears jeans and a T-shirt, having clearly changed from his hospital scrubs to street clothes.

He holds his hands in front of his chest, palms facing each other. His brows furrow in concentration as he stares at the space between his palms.

Smythe talks in a tone two levels above a mutter. Despite me standing in the entranceway to the living room, I can't hear him well enough to make out his words.

Light flares between Will's hands. His gaze turns to Smythe, happiness and surprise mixing together. Until the light extinguishes. The glee escapes from Will, deflating his excited expression as if he opened a present expecting a thousand dollars and instead received a bag of coal.

"Whatcha doing?"

Both men jump at my voice. What do you know? It has to be the first time I've ever surprised Smythe. Put that one down on my list of things not happening every day.

Smythe recovers first, gesturing at Will as he half-turns toward me. "Will is learning to form an energy ball."

Cool. "Can I sit and learn too?"

"Won't work with you." He shakes his head. "Sorry."

Well, crap. "You sure? Hi, Will. Nice car."

Smythe raises a brow. "Of course I'm sure."

"Hi, yourself," Will speaks at the same time. "And thanks."

"Can I go look at it?"

"Sure." He digs the keys out of his pocket, pitching

them to me. "Don't drive off."

Score! I catch the keys and scurry out the door.

After an ooh and ahh session, complete with a copious amount of petting, I return the keys to Will, breaking his concentration. Since sweat trickles down his cheek and his brow furrows into permanent lines, I'm pretty sure he doesn't mind the break. Smythe, though, is of an opposite opinion, judging from the glare he throws my way.

I shrug and smile. "You guys ready for dinner?"

"You cooked something?" Will's eager expression makes me feel bad for my next sentence.

"Nah. I thought we could order pizza."

"Sure." Smythe stands, reaches in his pocket and pulls out his wallet. He digs around and pulls out some bills, which he waves at me. "I'll pay."

"You don't—" Will starts speaking, but stops when I shake my head at him.

"Thanks." I reach for the bills, looking Smythe in the eyes as my fingers brush against his. A simple touch, but warmth spreads through me, releasing memories of our short time together.

Yeah, I want him. I need to swallow my pride and not let anger rule my heart. Easier said than done. Especially when I'm hungry and want dinner.

I slip the bills into my wallet and carry my purse into my bedroom before returning to the kitchen. Using my phone, I punch in our order for pizza.

As soon as I sign off the pizza ordering site, T and Eloise portal into the living room, shocking Will into dropping his energy ball onto my couch. Smoke swirls as the stench of burning fabric fills the air. Smythe snaps his fingers and the stench and smoke disappear.

I release a sigh of relief. No new couch for me. At least I assume that's what the vanishing smoke means. To be sure, I speed walk to the couch. Yep, Smythe fixed the burn. He's the best. Maybe I should cut him some slack. I lean over the back of the couch, wrap my arms around his shoulders and squeeze. He stiffens for a second then relaxes, patting my arms as his head rests on my shoulder.

"Gin?" T's voice snags my attention from Smythe to my twin.

"Hey. Sorry. Burning couch." I tilt my head toward the former burn as I release my hold on Smythe. "How'd it go?"

"Who's he?" T points to Will with the hand not holding Eloise's palm.

So that's how it was now.

I clear my throat to cover a chuckle. "Sorry. T and Eloise, met Dr. Will Wunderliech. T, Will went to high school with us and is one of the docs who works with me in the ER. Will, this is my twin, T, and the Agency healer, Eloise. Do you remember T from high school?"

T and Eloise step forward, dropping their held hands.

"Hey."

"Hello."

Will stands, shaking hands, no longer surprised by their sudden appearance. He squints at T. "I remember you."

"Yeah. I remember you too. You were always nice to my sister."

"Well," I clap my hands together. "Now that we have that settled. Tell us what you discovered at the Agency."

Eloise stares at Smythe for a second too long, head tilted. She releases a breath and nods. Guess he told her she could talk in front of Will. At least I assume we can talk in front of Will.

"It went okay," T says. "Didn't find a ghost."

"You spent the whole day there and didn't see a ghost?" Smythe raises a brow.

T shrugs. "It must've been hiding."

"These things take time." Eloise pats T's shoulder.

"Seriously?" I mirror Smythe's one brow up expression. "You didn't see a ghost?"

T glares at me. "Seriously."

But I peek inside his mind where a ghost resides, front and center, no digging around needed. A ghost. At the Agency.

Liar.

Get out of my head.

Since he doesn't block me, I assume his threat is nothing more than rhetoric. Wiping all expression off my face—no sense in giving away our convo to my uber-observant mentor—I shoot T a stare.

Make sure Smythe doesn't see inside your noggin.

Stay out and he won't.

Conversation between Eloise, Smythe, and Will floats around us, but I pay it no attention. If they talk amongst themselves, then they won't realize T and I carry on our own conversation.

A way more interesting conversation.

Does Eloise know?

Red splashes his cheeks. "I need a beer. Anyone else want one?"

"Sure," Will says, but Smythe and Eloise shake their heads, continuing their talk on what sounds like a demon discussion.

Interesting, but not enough to stay. Why would T lie about the ghost? Only one way to find out. I follow him into the kitchen.

T, does she know you saw a ghost?

He yanks open the fridge, pulls out three beers, sets one on the counter, and hands one to me. He answers as he twists off the top and takes a gulp. Speaking while swallowing poses no problem for telepathy.

No. Not yet. I'll tell her. More like ask her to go back. The place is crazy rich. Did you see the gold chandeliers?

Yes, they are and yes, I did, but we aren't talking about the money hanging off the walls. Why didn't you say anything to Eloise? She brought you there to see if there were ghosts you could talk to about the demon. I give him my best nurse's glare, the one reserved for people who avoid tasks they find hard.

He swallows, blows out a long breath and glances at the floor then back to me. *Wanted to make sure I could handle it.*

Handle it?

You know. Talk to the ghost. Without freaking out. Baby steps, Gin, baby steps.

Seriously? You didn't freak out when Blake popped in for a visit.

He raises a brow.

Okay, maybe you got a little sweaty and pale, but—

Yeah, it doesn't look cool, you know. He glances toward the other room. *She might not think pale and sweaty looks good on me.*

I can't avoid the eye roll. *This isn't speed dating. We are trying to kill a demon who's taking over the*

Agency.

Okay, okay. Don't freak. He takes a long swallow of beer. *I plan on having her take me back tomorrow. The ghost wasn't bad. Was female. Looked like she wanted to say something. She was surprised I could see her. Guess mediums aren't as common as mages in the building.*

That's why Eloise wanted you to help.

I am helping. Geez. We'll go back tomorrow. I'll go tell her now.

Please. I gesture toward the healer in a "get on with it" motion. *The sooner we destroy this demon, the better. Can you image what would happen if a demon ran the Agency? It could control us* Justitians.

He rolls his eyes, takes another long pull on the bottle. *I'm going. Right now. We'll go tomorrow. I'll call in sick again.*

Once he walks out of the room with Will's beer, I look at the bottle in my hands, condensation wetting my palms. Should I drink this? I relapsed recently. On the other hand, it's beer, not whiskey. I've never given up beer. Beer isn't relapsing.

Besides, I'm no longer as upset as the night I pulled out the bottle of whiskey, swallowing it down to relieve the guilt consuming my thoughts. Guilt still needles me, but the reality is Donny was destined to become a minion.

Yes, I should have noticed what was happening with him and Rahab before the last minute and convinced him to ignore the demon. Yes, I could have paid more attention to his exact location before I swung my sword, therefore avoiding his death.

But, he would've accepted Rahab's minion "gift"

no matter what I did, which meant eventually his death would've been by my hands. Of course, then he would've been a minion, not a human, but still. The result would be the same.

All that to say, I shouldn't feel guilty. And if I don't feel guilty, then there's no reason to ban beer on the off chance I might relapse again. I'm no longer as upset. I only hit the hard stuff when upset.

I take another look at the beer bottle. No problem. It's not whiskey and I'm not drinking to ease guilt. Everything's all good.

Decision solved, I twist the top and take a long pull of the fizzy liquid. I love beer.

The doorbell rings. Pizza time.

Smythe tips the delivery guy, takes the pizza boxes, and walks into the kitchen, everyone trailing behind him, hungry wolves on the scent of a deer. I pass out plates, napkins, and glasses. It's not until after everyone helps themselves, carrying plates and drinks to the table, that I notice Will stands in the hall to my bedroom, staring into space.

A plate with pizza poking out from under it lies upside down beside him on the floor. The pizza might not be the best in the world but it wasn't bad enough to dump on the floor.

Then Will drops to his knees, hands clasped over his ears, his eyes squeezed shut as if in agony.

Chapter Twenty-One

What the hell? None of us were talking loud enough to warrant his reaction. Nor did we have heavy metal turned up full blast. What was wrong with him?

I shove my plate full of pizza onto the counter. After catching Smythe's eye and gesturing to Will, I take a cautious step toward my downed friend. A ruffle of air, followed by a hint of warmth, brushes my back as Smythe steps right behind me. The happy-chatty noise in the kitchen dies.

I squat and place a hand on Will's shoulder. "Will?"

His eyes open, whites shining bright against his pale cheeks. Terror lances his gaze as a whimper escapes his lips. Definitely not a good sign. "Make it stop." His high-pitched cry stabs my heart.

I grab his wrist, skin on skin, using my empath ability to delve deep into his head. His emotions flood my senses: fear, anguish, guilt. Oh, the guilt. So many deaths. So much guilt. So much shame. So like me. Crimson and ebony waves batter my legs where I stand on a dark shore. A voice echoes, filling the air with a deep calming tone, lulling me with a false peace.

"Come to me. End your suffering."

No wonder my friend cringes upon the floor. A red wave slams into my leg, driving anger inside me, fueling a simmering rage. The damn demon of despair hides out in Will's mind, beckoning my friend to destruction, to death. Hate to tell Perdix, but he's messed with the wrong person. He's going down.

And I am the agent of his destruction.

Right after I figure out how to kill a demon who projects himself into another's mind.

I glance at my wrist, but the *justitia* remains a bracelet. Dammit. It makes sense; this is in Will's head, not a real ocean of water and waves, but infuriating nonetheless. How the hell am I supposed to kill a projection of a demon? Not the flesh and black-blooded demon, but a projection, an image, an illusion.

"Will!" My cry goes unanswered in the crashing of the ocean against the dark shore. "Will!"

This time he explodes from the waves like a breaching whale, landing in a stance beside me, his dry clothes incongruent with ocean exposure. Only in his imagination could he remain dry after a dunk in the waves.

"Get it away from me, Gin! Do something!" He slaps his hands over his ears, mimicking his physical self, his eyes pleading with me to end the torture.

I grab his upper arms. "It'll be okay. Don't worry. I'm here." Lying words, I have no idea if it'll be okay. I will try. But how? What do I do? How do I stop this demon from killing Will?

A switch flips inside my brain, illuminating an idea, a strange, dangerous idea, an instinct deep inside a primitive part of my brain. The concept is frightening, ripe with all sorts of ways to go wrong. Horribly wrong. But since it's the only idea offering a possible solution, I grab onto it with a death grip. Nothing left except to try. I refuse to let this demon hurt Will.

Acting on instinct, I move my hands to either side of his face, forcing my essence deeper into his mind, trying to trace the demon back to its lair.

Colors flash, each one a thought, an emotion, but I ignore them, focusing on the one item out of place in a mind ripe with feelings. A circular path disappearing into the distance. Wind batters my body, swirls in tightening eddies of a repellant barrier as I step closer. With an effort leaving me sweating, I step onto the path. Finally.

My relief is short-lived as a force grabs me, carrying me at lightspeed, as if I'm in a wormhole, spinning round and round. I land face down on a dirty, mold-stained carpet. Rolling to my side in self-defense of an impending allergy attack, I stare in growing horror at my hand.

My translucent hand. Completely see-through. Like I'm a ghost. I twist my hand back and forth, continuing to see the gray carpet instead of my expected flesh. Okay. Don't panic. No panicking allowed. I cannot run screaming from, well, where am I?

A quick glance around the room and I gasp, but make no sound. A weirdness I store for later. I'm in the abandoned for-sale house in my neighborhood. The one Smythe and I checked out earlier in the week. The one with the faded demonic trails.

Panic gives way to determination as my attention zeroes in on the other person in the room. Not a person, make that a demon. Heat flushes through my system, the anger tensing my muscles, speeding my pulse. Perdix stands before me, flesh and blood, not an illusion. His eyes are closed, his lips forming low-toned words recognizable to one who suffered through his attack.

Come to me and I will give you peace.

Bullshit. I can stop him. Now. Before he hurts another person. Before he kills Will.

I scramble to my feet, drawing my arm back, ready to charge. Except no sword juts from the *justitia*.

Despite being in a three-foot proximity to a demon, the *justitia* remains a bracelet.

What the hell? Without a sword, I'm next to useless in a demon fight. Why hasn't it changed? What's wrong with the thing?

I close my eyes, trying to locate the purple energy of the entity lying along my nerves. It's there, but faded. Seriously faded.

Justitia? Since I can't pronounce its actual name, *justitia* will have to do.

Wrong, wrong, wrong. Its voice drifts through my mind, riding a breeze of confusion. *Not me. Not you.*

My chest tightens. *Change into a sword.*

Wrong, wrong, wrong. Not me. Can't. Can't.

What do you mean, you can't? There's a demon three feet away!

Not me. Not you. Not real. In house. Not here. There.

Spit sticks in my throat. *So we can't kill Perdix?*

Not real. Can't kill. No sword.

Please, God, no. I'm right in front of the bastard. An easy kill. If I only had a sword. I have to stop him before he convinces Will to end his life. But how, when I'm as transparent as a spirit? A random thought brushes against my brain. Maybe all those people ended their lives to make the demon shut up. Maybe they didn't want to die, they wanted Perdix to stop talking in their minds.

A good thought, but one that fails to help me solve the problem at hand. *Focus, Gin, focus.* Clearly, I'm unable to kill Perdix in my current invisible, see-through form. Only in my physical body can the *justitia* activate into a demon-killing sword. I need to return to my body. Then I can tell Smythe where the demon is and we can come back and fry his ass.

But how?

Again, I act on instinct. My apparent modus operandi for the day. If I came here by following the demon's psychic connection to Will, in theory, I should be able to return to Will by following the same path. Sounds logical. Except the only way I see to do it is to hop into the demon.

Hopefully my brain won't hemorrhage from touching the thing, its evil overloading my empathic ability.

Not real. Won't hurt. The *justitia* confirms my hope.

Please, God, let the entity be right.

Before I can think better of it, I step to the demon. Taking a deep breath while praying this instinct wouldn't kill me, I slap my hands on either side of his face. And remain standing, no brain hemorrhage. Yes! Score one for the empath.

Perdix stiffens when I force my ghostly form through his flesh into his head. Colors swirl in a dizzying pattern. Lucky for me the curving path comprises the entire landscape of his mind, making it impossible to miss. Once my foot steps on the path, the circling, flashing lights carry me at hyper speed back to Will.

Please, God, let it be Will I land in.

Instead of Will's mind, I'm thrown into my body. My body inside Will's consciousness, that is. Will gasps as I land on my butt in the surf. He recovers quick, offering me his hand. Despite being in the water, I remain dry. Strange, but nice.

The reverberating voice negates my relief.

Come to me. I will give you peace.

"It didn't work." Will drops his head, his voice laced with panic.

"Yes, it did."

His head pops up, eyes wide as he draws in a deep breath. "It did?"

"Gin!" Smythe's voice drowns out the demon's, halting my reply.

Smythe! Wake me up! Would he hear me? Would he know what to do?

My body moves, as if shaken by an unseen hand. More like a mage's hand on my physical self. Yep, Smythe heard me and clearly knows what to do to get me to wake.

Come to think of it—apparently multiple jumps into different consciousnesses hindered the ability to think straight—I know how to wake up without his help. How to stop being inside Will's head. All I have to do is let go of Will.

Once I release my grip on his physical body, my consciousness will return to my body. Then I can tell Smythe where the demon is so we can portal to the bastard and whack off its head.

No problem. I got this.

"Will." I talk over Smythe's voice, which still calls me, a thread of tension saturating his words. "Hang in there. I know where the demon is and we'll go get him. Don't give in. Okay? Don't give in."

He nods, hands over his ears. "It's loud."

"I know, man, I know. Just hang in there, all right?"

"Hurry."

Closing my eyes, I imagine my fingers releasing their grip on Will's wrist, imagine my hand resting beside his but not touching. *Let go, let go, let go.*

With a gasp, I land in my body. My physical, solid body.

"Gin!" Strong hands squeeze my arms, give me a little shake, although not as hard as it felt inside Will's consciousness.

I'm back!

I draw in a deep breath. The scent of pepperoni pizza fills my nose. Ah. Home. Opening my eyes, I lock my gaze onto the side of Smythe's face, as he stares at where my hand rests next to Will's wrist. His gaze hops to mine, worry bleeding into relief. Then he grabs me a tight hug, a quick hug, releasing me before I can wrap my arms around his waist. Dammit.

Will lies crumpled beside me, curled into the fetal position, hands pressed against his ears. A tingle on the back of my neck alerts me to T and Eloise's close presence. Under normal circumstances, I'd let T know I was okay. His worry and fear leave an acrid scent in my nose, twist into an ache behind my sternum. But these aren't normal circumstances. Smythe needs to know the demon's location so we can stop him before he escapes.

Or kills Will.

I touch Smythe's arm. "I know where the demon is, but we have to move now."

Chapter Twenty-Two

When I said, "move now," I didn't expect Smythe to move quite so fast.

"The abandoned house?"

I nod, shocked by his mind-reading abilities without me aware of him being in my head. A happening that surprises me no matter how often it occurs. One of these days I'm going to learn how to tell when he sifted through my memories.

Smythe opens a portal, grabs my hand and yanks me through the passage before I can say: "howdy" or "good-bye" to Eloise and T. But I'm not complaining. The sooner we kill Perdix, the better. We land in the backyard of the demon-lair house in the darkening light of evening. Insects chirp as a cool breeze ruffles my hair. A dull roar from the closest large road sounds in the background, an accompanying duet to nature's symphony.

"Couldn't you land us inside the house?" Why land outside in the dark when inside gives us a quicker route to Perdix?

Smythe raises a brow, letting me know that option was a tactical mistake. "This way we have the element of surprise."

I lower my voice to a barely-there whisper. "But if we portaled right next to him, it would also have been a great element of surprise."

"Yes," he pitches his voice low like mine, "except you take too long to adjust after portaling. We might have surprised him by landing next to him, but you would have paused, giving him the advantage. This way you have time to adjust."

"I do not—" My protest dies on my lips as I realize he was right. Stepping out of the space-cold portal always took me a second to shake off the frigid air. Only a second. Okay, maybe a couple of seconds. A couple of seconds was all a demon needed to attack, to gain the upper hand, to win the fight.

Smythe was right. Again. Dammit.

"Fine. You might have a point. In my defense, those portals are freezing."

"Are you ready to kill a demon?"

I gesture to the house. "Lead on, oh master."

"It's mentor. Or guardian. Or mage." One side of his lips curls up. "Although, I do like the sound of master."

I roll my eyes, give a little head shake. "Get a move on. We don't have all night."

His wink sends tingles racing along my limbs, a reaction completely out of place for the situation. By the time I recover, he stands at the back door, muttering a spell. I jog to catch up, reaching him as he opens the thing enough for us to squeeze through without the tell-tale door squeak. A miasma of damp stench swirls in the air. I clamp a hand over my mouth and nose in self-defense. No wayward mold spores finding a new home in my sinuses.

Yuck. Where's a house flipper when you need one?

The dirty, gray carpet muffles our footsteps as we walk toward the room where the demon tries to entice

Will. With a small pop, the *justitia* forms into a sword, a welcome relief.

You real, me real. Kill demon. Excitement weaves through the entity's voice straight into my nerves, fueling my eagerness to rid the world of another demon.

Can you give me super-speed again? Like you did with the minion in Kathy's office?

A low rumbling chuckle spreads through my nerves. *Me give speed. You kill demon.*

Sounds like a plan to me.

We sneak down the hall, me in front, Smythe so close his breath ruffles my hair. The master bedroom door hangs halfway open, allowing us a clear view of Perdix, who stands back to us, facing a window. Despite his warped reflection in the glass panes, it's evident his eyes are closed. His lips move but no sound escapes. Besides us, he's the only one in the house. No minions to be found.

Which is odd. Usually a demon surrounds itself with minions.

Maybe he's too busy killing humans to turn one into a minion. You'd think he'd have protection in place, a guard, minions to offer their own lives in defense of the big, bad demon.

Why am I complaining about the intricacies of demon defense systems? No minions mean my sole focus stays on Perdix, leading to a quicker kill.

In theory.

Focused on enticing his latest victim, Will, Perdix misses hearing our approach. Unfortunately, his eyes pop open, his gaze meeting mine in the reflection off the window, right as I swing at his neck. He leaps out of the way, turning to face us, gaze shifting between me and my mage. A sinister smile spreads his lips wide.

I am not scared of his chill-inducing smile. Really. I am not.

"Ah." The deep tone of his voice crawls like spiders across my skin. "A visit from the illustrious *Justitian* and her somewhat capable guardian. Whatever have I done to deserve such a pleasure?"

Pushing my insecurity out of the way, I narrow my eyes, point my sword at the demon. "I think you know." I step to the side in a blur of movement, trying to get in a swing, but he mirrors my movements. Smythe stands in the doorway, waiting for the action to begin before deploying his life-saving magic skills.

"You think you can defeat me this time. You think by bringing your guardian you can win. You think I won't kill you because you belong to another. You think wrong."

Why is it demons prefer bragging to attacking? They seem unable to perform without taunts, threats, and enough bravado to con a conman. Maybe it comes with living in Hell.

Ignoring the ego-inflated demon's words, I dash forward, sword drawn back.

The stupid demon disappears, only to reappear behind me, giving me a shove. I stumble forward, but thanks to Smythe's magic, land on a thin, but cushiony invisible mat. The entity along my nerves shrieks in my head.

Demon move faster than me!

Great. My super-speed means little against Perdix. At least Smythe's here to help. Thank god for guardian mages.

A roll, a turn, and I face the demon. Another shit-eating smile spreads across his face as he steps to the side, offering me a clear view of Smythe. Who clasps his hands over his ears, dropping to the ground in classic there's-a-demon-in-my-head pose.

My breath hitches. *Oh my god, not him too.*

Perdix chuckles. A bead of sweat trickles down my spine.

"Think I cannot fight you and destroy him? Think I am weak?" Pure malice taints his laugh. "I will destroy you. And him. And anyone else I see fit. I will be ruler of Hell and all within it. Not your thrice cursed master."

What the hell is he talking about? Besides the destroying part. That I get. No time to puzzle the answer. Without Smythe, I'm on my own against this demon. If experience has taught me anything, Gin versus demon equals me being screwed.

I glance to the crumpled form of my guardian. Pain squeezes my heart. Pain mixed with a healthy dose of rage. How dare Perdix try to kill the man who's my mentor, my friend, my lover? Rage wipes clean the remaining anger I feel over Smythe's betrayal. The last thing I want is for Smythe to be hurt, for him to give in to the demon's will, for him to die.

Only one way I know of to avoid that fate.

Kill the damn demon.

Which means I need to get over my doubts, my feelings of being screwed, my lack of confidence. I will take down Perdix. I will kill the fucking demon before he kills Smythe. And I will revel in his death.

Keeping an eye on the chatty demon who continues his tirade about my destruction and him becoming ruler of Hell, I do the one thing I swore never to do during a demon fight.

Call T.

T! Help! Smythe is down!

A wave of rage batters the barriers between my twin and I. *Where are you?*

The house for sale on Florida Avenue. Only one on the block. Hurry! I don't know how long I can hold off this demon.

Be right there.

He slams our connection closed a second before Perdix rushes me. Guess I wasn't paying as close attention to the demon as I thought. The tip of a sword he pulled from who knows where slices my arm, drawing blood.

Damn, that hurt.

One of these days I'm going to show up to a demon killing in the leather pants and black shirt Smythe gave me to fight Agramon. I might still get cut, but at least my good clothes won't be ruined.

Ignoring the throbbing pain in my arm, I draw back my sword to attack. The *justitia* blocks my pain receptors, allowing me an agony-free swing. The demon leaps out of the way, only to return my swing with one of his own. Slash, duck, spin, counter. We both move so fast the room fades to a swirl of white walls and gray carpet. Sweat drenches my shirt as we parry.

The edge of my blade slices through his sword arm, cutting deep into his flesh, black blood marring his sleeve. He roars, his sword dropping with a dull thud onto the floor. I pull my arm back for the killing blow.

Halfway through the swing my body lifts from the ground, thanks to a demon anti-gravity move. With a flick of his hand, I fly through the air, crash into the dry wall, and tumble onto the nasty carpet.

Pain rips into my ribs, spreading across my torso, stealing my breath. I'm pretty sure I broke something, but once again the *justitia* shuts down the pain receptors along my nerves, returning me to a functional state. More like a barely functional state. Despite the lack of pain, my body shakes as I roll, as it takes two tries to sit upright. Coppery wetness fills my mouth. I spit blood onto the filthy carpet.

Great. Now what in my body is beyond broken?

No time to worry. Padded footfalls step closer.

"Had enough?"

I stare at the demon, hock another wad of blood on the carpet. The cackle in his laugh scrapes along overly sensitized nerves. Smythe continues to writhe on the floor, the agony written on his face, in his curled position, deepens the ache in my chest. Muscles quivering, I rise to my feet.

Perdix might knock me down, but no way will I allow him to mess with Smythe. The mage has saved my ass too many times for me to give in to my pain, freaking over serious blood-inducing injuries.

Red dots stain my vision as I rush Perdix.

The demon flicks a couple of fingers, the energy blast lifting me airborne, arms and legs pinwheeling, a broken puppet cut loose from its strings. Air rushes past my face as the opposite wall grows nearer. I wince, preparing for the hit, but instead of the wall, I land on a cushion of air. The moment the mat catches my flying body, the roar of an injured animal explodes into the small room, reverberating in the empty space.

Goosebumps prickle my skin. The mat floats me to the floor with the gentleness of a feather. As soon as my feet hit the ground, I turn, knowing without seeing who made the cry of anguish and anger.

T stands beside Eloise in front of a downed Smythe and Will. Will? Why was Will here curled on the ground in a fetal position? Shouldn't he be at my house? I shove the thought aside, focusing on my irate twin. Arms held to his sides at shoulder height, eyes rolled so far back in his head only the whites show, his continued curdling yell stops Perdix in his tracks.

A cold burst of air blows through the room, dropping the temperature at least twenty degrees. My breath comes in small puffs of vapor. The hair on the back of my neck stands at attention. Blood drips off my lip and I wipe it away with the back of my left hand.

Wisps of fog swirl into the room, aiming for T, circling around my twin in a dance of attraction. My fuzzy brain takes a moment to connect the dots. T wasn't hollering to give me a fighting advantage. He was calling multiple ghosts.

And they were obeying.

A small smile turns my lips as tingles spread across my skin. T finally opened himself to his kick-ass ability.

Perdix turns pale. "What are you doing?"

"Killing you, bitch." I spit out the words, along with a good deal of blood. The sooner we kill this demon, the quicker Eloise can heal me.

Silence spreads through the room as my twin stops yelling, punctuated by the heavy breathing of a sweating demon. T brings his hands together with a loud clap, palms touching, arms pointing at the demon. Air crackles as the wisps of vapor stream straight through Perdix.

The demon roars, batting at the air as if slapping away mosquitoes. Too bad for him, the ghosts ignore his feeble attempts to dissuade their attack.

Ghosts whirl around me, brushing my skin, each touch eliciting racing tingles which spread until shivers rack my body. At least they don't arrow through me like they do Perdix. The demon flails at the whirling ghosts, screeching each time one pierces his body.

Pointing my sword forward, I creep toward the frightened demon. Thank goodness the *justitia* blocks pain receptors. Otherwise, I would never be able to draw my arm back for a killing blow. Grasping my right wrist with my left hand for stability, I swing with all my strength. At the last second, before steel meets flesh, the demon looks at me, eyes wide, fear written in their depths.

Good-bye, sucka. The *justitia* slices through the demon's neck like a scalpel through flesh, clean and smooth. Except for the black blood spattering the walls and me like a macabre abstract expressionist painting.

Perdix's head and body fall in two different directions. His body crumples to the floor while the head rolls to a stop against the wall, black blood trailing in its wake. A flash of light followed by a pop and the body disappears into fine black silt. Good thing a cleanup crew exists.

For another moment, the ghosts circle the pile of silt like vultures waiting for a meal before vanishing. The room warms with their leaving, my breath no longer visible. With a tiny pop, the *justitia* returns to bracelet form.

Smythe releases his grip on his head, starts to straighten to his knees, pain easing from his expression

as he draws in a deep breath. He looks straight at me.
"What happened?"

Chapter Twenty-Three

Instead of answering, my attention snaps to my twin, who sways an instant before he crumples to the floor. Smythe can deduce what happened on his own.

"T!" I race to his side, dropping to my knees beside him.

Eloise joins me, kneeling on his other side, hands brushing mine aside as she performs a healing scan.

"What's wrong?" I reach for T, pulling my hands back when Eloise shoots me a glare.

"Energy drain."

Heavy, slow steps sound as Smythe walks to us. He stands behind Eloise, peering over her shoulder, hands on his hips, his face showing concern, no evidence of his ordeal apparent. Behind him, Will leans against the wall, rubbing a hand across his forehead as if to soothe a headache.

"What happened?"

This time I answer Smythe, my gaze never leaving my twin. "We killed the demon."

He exaggerates a sigh. "How?"

I gesture to T, happy to note color returning to his face as healing magic streams into his body. Eloise rocks.

"T called ghosts who darted into the demon. They created enough of a distraction for me to slice off his head."

"You look hurt."

My gaze meets Smythe's. Lines crease his forehead, drawing his eyebrows together. I look hurt? I glance at my arm, at the blood streaking my shirt, remember my flight into the wall. The only reason I remain upright is due to the *justitia* blocking all pain. I should be unconscious. I should want an immediate healing to stop the room from dancing a whirl.

Instead I'm more concerned about T.

Eloise touches my arm, skin on skin, but no wayward emotions crash into me. She's learned to keep her thoughts to herself. Unfortunately.

"Oh, my." Her eyes widen. "You need my help more than T does. Lie down." She points at the floor, as if there was any other horizontal option.

I wrinkle my nose. Hopefully she'll rid me of the cooties I'm bound to catch lying on the filthy surface. Although, why take the chance? Yes, my ribs are broken and blood continues to pool in my mouth, but I'd rather lay on my couch to be healed than risk this floor. Having my knees touch it was bad enough.

"I can wait until we get back home."

Eloise tilts her head. Her eyes narrow. "There is nothing on the carpet to bother you. Now lie down."

Either she possesses a compulsion spell that puts Smythe's to shame, or I have a sudden change of heart. Without further question I do as she says, stretching out on the grime and praying for the germs to leave me alone.

She touches my shoulder and the room spins away, the scene changing into blue sky dotted with fluffy white clouds. I float on an ocean, the low current bobbing me up and down, up and down, a relaxing motion calming my soul. Yep, Eloise still has that healing touch.

All too soon, the ocean fades, the room with its dull overhead light coming into focus. T sits beside me, normal coloring and a worried look on his face that morphs into a grin as my lids flutter open.

Low voices in the background clue me in others besides the five of us are in the house. The cleanup crew? To have a private moment alone with my twin, I speak telepathically, while remaining flat on my back.

Are you okay?

Yeah. You?

I draw in a deep breath. *Yep. How did you do it? The ghosts, I mean.*

His brow furrows as his gaze glazes with remembered horror. *I saw you on the ground. Bleeding. Don't know how I did it. I wanted the fucking demon dead. Something inside me snapped, and, well, it just happened. Drained the hell out of me.*

I'm glad you're okay. You scared me when you dropped out cold.

He glances down, back to me. *I enjoyed it. All the power. Controlling all those ghosts. Who the hell can do that, you know? Directing them, having them enter the demon, who the fuck knew it would happen? Ghosts beat demons.* He shakes his head. *It was more than talking to them. Wasn't at all like the time with our father. That was pure ghost talking. This, this was different. Does it make me a horrible person if I enjoyed it?*

No. Not at all. I answer without thinking. Does a power grab make one bad? Only if the grab is for yourself. Using ghosts to kill a demon benefits humanity. All good. No problem. Besides, T was a good person.

Sure, he had his quirks, like falling for women with double D's and a lack of brains—Eloise being excluded from those certain traits—but he has been a stabilizing force throughout my life, the person who always had my back. I love my twin.

If he wants to shoot ghosts through demons, it makes him a good person in my book, not a bad one. *Killing a demon is always a good thing as far as I'm concerned.*

Maybe I should go with you more often when you fight demons.

Not so sure I want you anywhere close to being hurt.

Same here. He grabs my hand, gives it a squeeze. *Come on, let me help you up. They're finished cleaning the room and waiting for us to leave.*

He pulls me to my feet. Spots dance in front of my eyes as dizziness swamps me. I grab onto his arm to stay standing. Flat to upright too fast tends to cause my head to spin. Once the room stops whirling, I release my grip. T gives my palm a squeeze before dropping my hand.

"Does this mean you are going to tell Eloise you saw a ghost?"

He crosses his arms. "I said I'd ask her to take me back."

"So it's a yes?" I grin. He glares.

But only for a second. Then his grin matches mine. "Yeah. Maybe talking to them won't be so bad. Maybe I can meet more of our relatives."

"That's the spirit." I give his arm a playful whack.

"Ha. Get it? Spirit?"

He rolls his eyes. "Give it up Gin. You aren't as punny as you think you are."

"Whatever. You know you like it."

"Keep on deluding yourself." He pats my shoulder. I shake my head.

"Come on. Let's go home."

We follow the voices down the hall. Smythe, Eloise, Will and the cleanup crew stand in the living room, their hushed conversation ending at our approach.

Eloise steps forward with a smile creasing her face. "There's our demon killer. Better?"

I give her a hug. "Thank you. Again. Your healing rocks."

She pats me twice on the back, a silent request for me to release her, which I do.

"Glad you are up and around." Smythe touches my arm, his gaze drawing me in, drowning me in the depths of his concern. Deeper emotions cross his face, shadows of desire.

Yeah, I forgive him. Maybe I should continue being pissed, but life is too short to live without him being more than my guardian mage. I need to tell him how I feel when we get back to my place.

Provided I can think of a way to approach the issue without seeming like all I want is a bedmate.

For now, I offer him a grin and a hug. "I'm glad to see you up and about too." I turn to Will, who stands apart, a little awestruck, a lot uncomfortable.

I don't even need to touch him to get a read on his emotions. His wide eyes coupled with his hand running through his hair and continuing gaze hopping are clues enough.

My poor friend got a crash course in demon hunting.

I give him a hug too. He looks in desperate need of one. A quick touch on the back of his neck proves my suspicion: shock and awe.

"Glad you are okay, Will. Why did you come?"

"Didn't want to leave him alone." T slaps him on the back as I drop my arms from his waist. "Didn't want him doing anything rash with the demon messing with his head."

"Good decision. Although I'm not sure exactly what happened." Will pitches the last word almost like a question, as if he wants us to explain.

We don't. Maybe later. My stomach growls. For now, I want to get home to reheated pizza, a beer, and a discussion of how to storm the Agency. You know. A normal Friday night.

Chapter Twenty-Four

Eloise opens a portal and shuttles everyone except the cleanup crew to my kitchen. The pizza might not be hot, but the kitchen holds the delightful scent of pepperoni and tomato sauce. While everyone else grabs cold pizza, taking turns reheating it in the microwave, I go to my room to change clothes. Nothing like black demon blood to kill an appetite.

After changing into clean jeans and a T-shirt, I nuke my pizza and join the others at the table for a post-demon-killing wrap up. Since my beer is now warm, I stick the opened bottle in the fridge to cool off, grabbing a new replacement.

"Anyone else want a beer?" I hold up my bottle for a visual reference.

"Sure."

"Yes, please." Will echoes T's request, while Eloise and Smythe shake their heads.

Putting my plate and bottle on the counter, I grab beers from the fridge, deliver them to Will and T, grab my food and drink, and sit in the chair next to Smythe.

He pats my leg, fingers lingering a second too long for the touch to be a "hi, nice to see you." I grab his hand, give it a quick squeeze, the touch letting him know I feel the same. Next on my to-do list, have another chat with him about us.

Harder than it sounds. Why is it relationship

discussions tend toward the complicated? No wonder so many people end up at a relationship therapist. It's easier to ignore the elephant in the room wearing a pink tutu until it squashes you flat and dances on your bones. Then it's too late to say anything and you're filled with pain and frustration.

"Is this what you do every day, Gin?" Will's voice draws me out of my thoughts.

"Not every day. But, yeah, this is what I do as a *Justitian.* Hunt and kill demons and minions. Did it scare you?" A grin turns my lips.

A look of horror crosses Will's face. "Of course not!" Yep, no man alive admits to being scared. "I woke up once it was over. Are all demons so powerful?"

"Most demons don't invade your thoughts." Smythe sets his pizza on his plate as he answers Will. "You usually fight them in the flesh, not in your imagination."

Red tinges Will's cheeks. "I didn't do such a hot job of fighting it in my imagination."

"No one does." I look him in the eye. "He was the leader of the despair demons. The demon who killed your foster dad. He had eternity to practice killing people by invading their thoughts. By causing them to want to die. Don't beat yourself up over not getting in a punch."

Will nods. "Thank you for offing the one who killed Dad. Knowing you killed the demon is almost as good as killing it myself."

I tilt my beer his direction. "Any time. Happy to help."

Smythe pats my knee again, this time withdrawing

his hand much too fast.

"We are glad you are joining us." Eloise smiles in Will's direction.

"Especially now." Smythe shoves his chair back, grabs his plate, and refills it with pizza.

Will mimics him, talking as he waits for the microwave. "What's with now?"

"We suspect a demon lives in the Agency." I follow the guys to the pizza, T on my heels. Fighting Perdix worked up an appetite.

"The Agency is your boss, right?" Will sticks his plate in the microwave and sets the timer once Smythe pulls out his warm pizza.

"Yeah. It's the corporation overseeing the *Justitians* and mages who fight the demons and minions."

"The demon doesn't just live at the Agency," Eloise says, turning toward our voices. "I believe it wants to take over the Agency."

Will pulls his plate out, walks back to the table. "I'm new to this, but even I can see where that would be bad. What are you going to do about it?"

Beep! The dinger alerts me to my nuked pizza, and I pull it out while answering Will. "Kill it. What else?"

"It's more complicated than that." Smythe shakes his head, giving me a "really?" look.

Why doesn't he pop into my mind like usual? Maybe he's giving me alone time to decide if I want him back. Yep, we definitely need to have a conversation. Later. After we plot and scheme how to kill the Agency's live-in demon.

"We have to find the demon first," Eloise says.

A thought flits through my mind at her words. "I

know—" And then the thought vanishes, leaving everyone looking at me. But for a split second I knew who the Agency demon was. Until my mind stumbled over the knowledge. What was I thinking again?

"You know what?" Eloise asks.

"Nothing. Sorry. Go on." I wave a hand as a dull headache throbs against my skull. What was I thinking about the Agency demon? How to kill it? Right. That must've been it. How to track and kill it. My headache fades into nothing as the conversation continues.

"Where do you fit in?" Will tilts his head at T.

"I see ghosts." T glances at me for a second. "I'm a ghost talker. I can call them and make ghosts do what I want."

His sense of pride brushes my mind through our telepathic link, while his voice remains a steady, stating-the-facts tone.

"It's a rare ability." Smythe gives T his see-through stare, the one guaran-damn-teed to see straight into a person's mind, to read his soul. Could he fathom T's secrets? Delve into my twin's head like he did mine?

Learn the one secret we swore to keep until we died?

Probably.

Would I ever admit that secret to Smythe? Could I trust him enough to tell him?

Maybe. Probably.

But not today.

T shrugs, all no big deal, as if orchestrating ghosts was a daily occurrence.

A smile cracks Smythe's lips, an indication he probed deep enough into T's mind to learn my brother never called a ghost in his life. At least not in the way he did during the fight. Instead of calling T out, my mentor keeps the knowledge to himself.

"Okay," Will says as he turns to Smythe. "You told me my parents were mages. Do you know anything else about them?"

"Were your parents, Frank and Rachel Wunderliech?" Eloise leans forward, brows furrowed.

"Yes. Did you know them?"

She leans back, a shit-eating grin I normally associate with demons written on her face. "I did. They helped me steal Gin's *justitia* from the vault at the Agency. They promised to protect it."

Will's eyes widen. "Why would they do that?"

"Her *justitia* is powerful, more so than the others, for it can control the other *justitias*. In the right hands, or wrong as the case may be, Gin's *justitia* has the ability to make the other *justitias*, and therefore the *Justitians*, do its bidding."

According to what Eloise said earlier, she thought only demons can use my *justitia* to control the others. What if, unbeknownst to her, I have that power? What if there's a way for me to control my sword sisters? Do I even want to possess that much power? But I have no time to puzzle it out, as Eloise continues talking.

"It's an ability lost to the present. But the demons created these bracelets and it stands to reason they still remember the spell. If the *justitia* fell into demon hands, life as we know it would go to Hell. Literally. I learned a demon was in the Agency and took steps to ensure they would not get their hands on the *justitia*." She touches Will's arm. "I am sorry for your loss."

He pulls away, eyes narrow, lips pursed. A second later his anger deflates. "They knew what would happen if they were caught, didn't they?"

"They did. It was a risk they were willing to take."

"Even if it meant leaving me alone?"

"I am sorry, Will."

The rest of us remain silent, allowing Will to compose himself, to wipe away the tears threatening to spill.

Topic change time. "How do you propose we find the demon in the Agency?"

Eloise clears her throat. "Years ago, the last ghost talker said ghosts inhabited the Agency. I had hoped they continued to hang around."

"We can go back tomorrow and I'll have another look." T glances to me for a split second, a silent plea to keep my mouth shut. Outside of a grin attempting to twist my lips, I do as he wants.

Eloise nods. "We'll go tomorrow. Maybe our search will be successful and we'll find one of the ghosts."

My bet is on success. Seeing as there is definitely a ghost wanting to chat and a ghost talker now willing to listen.

"When you say years ago," Will's voice cracks and he clears it, "how many years do you mean?"

"Around the turn of the century."

"That's not too long ago."

Smythe shakes his head. "She means the turn of the last century."

Will's eyes widen. His pizza plops onto his plate. "Last century? You mean around 1900?" At Eloise's nod, his eyes narrow. "In other words, you don't have a real plan."

"It's a real plan." Will raises a brow at my words.

"It's as good as any other one."

"Seriously? This"—he waves a hand—"is how you track demons?"

"No." Smythe shakes his head. "We are more methodical. This is a special situation. Eloise has known about it for awhile, but hasn't always been able to trust others to help her find the demon."

"It's been years since I found mages to trust." Her voice lowers. "Since your parents. They saw the same thing I did. Suspected the same thing I did. And were willing to help."

"You just now trusted him?" Will points at Smythe.

Eloise flicks her gaze between the two mages as if she can see them. No surprise. She sees more than she admits. "I trusted Aidan, but needed to ascertain where his loyalties lay before I could ask for his help."

"What's that supposed to mean?" Smythe furrows his brow.

Eloise shrugs, her gaze focusing on my mentor. After a couple of tense, silent seconds, he nods.

Telepathy to the rescue. On the down side, the rest of us remain in the dark as to why Eloise didn't trust Smythe. I assume I can wheedle it out of him later. But Will looks confused as hell.

"Did you answer him?" Will stares at Eloise.

She smiles, one side of her lips twisting upward. "You are very curious."

"I am new to this and want straight answers."

I hate to tell him, but straight answers around the Agency and its employees are a rarity.

"All in good time, Will. All in good time."

Will shifts in his seat, eyes narrowing, his posture

one of a man gathering his thoughts before exploding with anger.

Smythe interrupts the growing tension, pushing his plate out of the way and leaning forward on his elbows. "What do you want Gin and I to do? Our job here is complete. We can help."

"Tomorrow? Nothing." Relief weaves through Eloise's tone. "Clearly you will be needed to take down the demon, but for tomorrow, you aren't needed. I'll take T and we'll continue to look for a ghost. Hopefully the ghost will tell us who to target."

"And then we'll move in and take them out."

Sounds easy in theory. I bet the actual taking out gets a lot more complicated.

Chapter Twenty-Five

Will leaves after dinner, upset over his parents, and the lack of our straight-shooting answers. I know this because I hug him good-bye, making sure I touch his skin for a foolproof empath reading. He's yet to be told about my touch-and-see ability and I have no plans to clue him in.

Eloise hugs us good-bye, her arms lingering around T's waist. And, yep, my twin wears a goofy grin on his face. Which makes a goofy grin appear on my lips, except mine is for a whole different reason.

He had feelings for the healer before Jackie's untimely death. Despite the obvious rush into another's arms, I'm happy for him. I can see him with Eloise in a way I never could with Jackie. T is a smart guy. Except when it comes to women. Maybe I should put that in the past tense since Eloise is a good catch.

Unless she's using my brother for her own machinations.

My gaze narrows on the healer. I like her. A lot. She has saved my ass more times than I can count and has become somewhat of a friend. But if she ever hurts my brother, she's dead.

Figuratively, speaking, that is. How the heck would I off a healer who can negate the Agency's wards?

Things won't come to that. I hope.

"I'll come tomorrow morning around nine. Good

night." With a circular wave of her hand, she opens a portal, disappearing into its depths.

"I'm exhausted." T yawns while scratching his stomach.

I give him a hug, feeling like an ass for not noticing the dark circles around his eyes, the sleepy expression in his eyes. Some nurse I am.

"Thank you for the assist. You did good today."

"Yeah, I did, didn't I?"

"Don't get all puffed up about it."

He gives me a kiss on my cheek. "I'm never puffed up. Sleep well."

"You too."

He walks into his room, shutting the door behind him, leaving Smythe and me standing in the living room. Alone. Needing to discuss the pink tutu-wearing relationship elephant.

No sense in putting off The Talk. Who knows when we'll have another chance.

Smythe rubs the back of his neck. "Guess I should be going."

I draw in a deep breath. No time like the present.

"We need to talk."

Four words men hate. The dreaded talk.

He pales, but nods, perching on the edge of the couch, hands palm down on his knees, gaze focused on his feet. I sit beside him, tucking one foot under the opposite knee, facing him.

Touching his arm, drawing his attention to mine, I clear my throat. Women hate The Talk, too.

"I forgive you."

His gaze jumps to mine, a fragile hope swimming in its depths. "Forgive and forget or just forgive?"

"Forgive. There's not a way to forget that cluster fuck of a fight." My tone hardens. Dammit. I didn't want to sound accusatory. I'm tired of being accusatory.

The hope in his eyes morphs into regret as he nods. "I'm sorry. Where do we go from here?"

Another throat clear as I force my gaze to meet his. "Where do you want to go? Is it over between us or do you want to salvage things?"

"You know the answer." He stares into my eyes, pausing a moment for emphasis, the truth of his coming words evident in his unwavering gaze. "You mean more to me than anyone else I've been with."

Yes! I rank higher than Samantha the blonde bitch mage. Not that there's a competition going on or anything. A smile creeps across my lips.

"I care about you too. Caring means trusting. Trusting the other not to run off."

"Sometimes the other runs off." His gaze grows distant.

A memory tickles my mind, an insight into why he acted like such an ass, a reason for his actions.

"What happened?" I know he had a girlfriend before we started working together, a *Justitian* girlfriend who died, but the details remain sketchy.

His gaze drops to his white-knuckled hands clutching his knees. After a long pause, he speaks, low and soft.

"Jennifer left me."

"The *Justitian*?"

He nods. "She cheated on me with a fellow mage. I was her guardian. When I heard the news, I got shit-faced. I mean, I loved her and thought she felt the same about me, but I was wrong." He draws in a deep breath.

"I was so drunk I couldn't help her when she needed me." Another deep breath. "It was my fault she died fighting a minion. I wasn't there for her."

I rest my hand on top of his. "I'm sorry."

He doesn't say anything, his chest rising and falling, as if the rhythm alone keeps shame to a minimum.

The fact my insight was correct gives me no happiness.

"When you saw me and Donny, you thought the same thing happened again, didn't you?"

He nods. "Yeah. But I didn't realize there was a demon."

Seriously? "You stormed right by it."

"I was so upset, I wouldn't have noticed a dinosaur dancing in front of me. I just wanted out of there."

"That helps." I squeeze his hand. "It upset me when you left since you wouldn't listen to me."

"And then you needed my help and I wasn't there."

"As I said, I forgive you. We can start over. Try to trust each other again." Now it's my turn to look at my lap while drawing in a deep breath. "I haven't been the most trustworthy person either. I've broken your trust." When I did what Zagan wanted. When I lied about it. When my actions told Smythe I'd turned to the side of the demons.

In all fairness to me, speaking out against the demon of lies and deceit proves harder than it sounds. I want to keep Zagan's secrets, even when it means breaking trust with my guardian. My *justitia's* friendship with the demon sends those vibes throughout our bond, making it impossible to differentiate between what the bracelet feels and my own emotions.

I need to jettison that reaction. I need to keep the trust with Smythe. I need to put my guardian above a demon.

Why is it so hard?

I swallow.

Smythe twists his palm until he holds my hand. "We can work on it together." His gaze grabs mine, pulling me into his inner depths, washing away the pain keeping us separated.

Together. Not apart. Not alone. Together. Once we make the decision, once we know we belong with the other, nothing will pull us apart. And yet, the decision is the hardest thing I've admitted. Harder than telling Smythe I lied for Zagan when the demon asked. Smythe is the one person I can see myself with forever. Making a relationship decision affecting the rest of my life proves difficult.

Even when I know it's the right one.

Woman up, Gin. Admit you want him the way he wants you. Forever.

I lean forward, meeting his lips halfway, speaking with an action destined to set me on a lifelong path. His lips move over mine, our tongues tangling with a preview of coming deeds, speaking in a language as old as time. His arms tighten around my waist, lifting, until I straddle his legs. But only for a moment and then he stands, carrying me with my legs wrapped around his waist to my bedroom where he kicks the door shut behind us.

*****

I wake with a warm arm draped across my waist, the heat from Smythe's body better than a blanket. A sense of belonging sweeps through me, a promise of life with another. We fit well together, curled on my bed, warm from fucking. A lifetime with this man will never be enough.

Right this instance, though, I need water. My dry throat cries for relief. Not only does fighting a demon work up an appetite, it appears it also works up a delayed thirst.

Lifting Smythe's arm, I roll away from his warmth, landing on my feet. The mattress squeaks, but he continues to sleep, his breath even. I want to kiss his brow, but doing so would lead to another sex-fest, thereby delaying my drink. At the moment I need water more than I need sex.

Grabbing my robe off the chair, I shove my arms into the armholes, and tie the belt around my waist. I pull the door closed behind me, not wanting to disturb Smythe. T's door is shut. Hopefully he didn't hear my horizontal action session. Unlike him, who couldn't care less who heard what, I prefer to keep things quiet from others in the house.

Except for tonight. Cementing a relationship can be a little loud.

I smile, remembering, as I walk into the dark kitchen. A glow from the streetlamp a door down illuminates the room, allowing me to grab a glass without turning on the light. After gulping down two glasses, I set the glass in the sink, and turn to go back to bed.

Only to come to a stop, hand over my pounding heart. My bracelet jitters a happy-happy dance on my wrist. Just who I wanted to see.

"Geez, Louise, scare a girl why don't you."

Zagan leans against the jamb between the living

room and kitchen, arms crossed, his t-shirt stretched tight against thick muscles, the white fabric seeming to glow in the partial light. A smile twists his lips, teeth gleaming bright. Sharp teeth. A shiver courses down my spine.

I cross my arms, mimicking his stance, trying to look tough while wearing a robe over my birthday suit.

"Ah, little *Justitian.* I am glad to see you."

"Cut the crap, Zagan. The last time you saw me you told me I was worthless."

"Merely words spoken in anger. Nothing more."

"Sounded like more to me."

His head tilts, his gaze probing my soul. "You are hurt by those words."

"Stupid, eh?" Why should a demon's words hurt me? And yet, his words sliced through my heart like a knife through skin.

He takes a step forward, dropping his arms, but I hold out a hand and he stops.

"Not stupid. You belong to me."

"Yeah. Right. Not happening."

"Already happened. But that is neither here nor there."

"Seriously?" Does he really mean it doesn't matter? At his glare, I swallow the rest of my words, refuse to quake in fear.

"As. I. Said. Neither here nor there. What matters is you won the fight."

"So what you're saying is you only like me if I win against a demon? If I kill your brethren? Are you crazy?"

One brow raises. "I am not crazy. Focused. But you know that, don't you? You understand focus. Focus brings you many things, does it not? When one remains focused, one achieves their wish. I am sorry my focus disturbed you."

"The hell? It was your words that disturbed me, not your focus." Dammit. Did I actually admit to a demon he upset me? What the hell is wrong with me?

"Words. Focus. Same—" His voice trails into silence. He sighs. "You are correct. They are not the same thing. My focus remains the same. You are part of the goal. The means to attain it. When you failed to kill Rahab, it was…difficult to accept."

"What you're saying is you only care about me if I help you reach your goal."

He slaps a hand over his chest, his brows rising with fake surprise. "I am hurt."

"Don't bullshit me. You are not and you know it."

He shrugs. "As you wish. Hurt might be a bit strong of a word. Know this, I care about you. As much as a demon can care about a human."

Scary thought. A little voice tells me his idea of caring and my idea of caring are polar opposite. When I care, it's because a person means something to me, a friend, a lover, and I hate to see them harmed. Zagan's idea of caring is self-serving. He cares because caring makes him reach his goal faster.

Whatever his goal might be.

And yet, his words warm my heart, give me meaning.

I'm so screwed up.

"What is your goal?"

His eyes narrow as he pauses, his normal smartass remarks silenced as he clearly wages an internal debate of what to tell me. I wait.

"And what will you do with this information?"

I tilt my head. "Should I do something with it?"

"You might decide you should. You might try to harm my goal. I am close. So close. Setback now would prove…unlucky."

Memories of the *justitia* assail my mind. Memories of multi-hued demons around a fire, plotting, scheming. I know his goal. His patience in achieving it. His scheme to see it through.

"You want control of Hell."

His eyes widen. His body stills. My heart thuds against my ribs, echoes in my ears, a discordant beat. Did I piss him off enough to harm me? Would he, could he, harm me?

Those thoughts vanish as he smiles his best shit-eating grin.

"Want to help me win?"

"How?" What would be the advantage of Zagan in charge of Hell, instead of whoever reigned? Who did reign? Lucifer?

"Defeat the strongest demons. You have already killed two. There are two more left, one of which is the strongest of all demons. Only your help can assist me in overthrowing this demon." His lips flatten.

Great. If the demon freaks Zagan, I can't image what the thing is like. Worse than Agramon, the leader of the fear demons? That was one scary-ass mother, the likes of which I never wanted to meet again.

"Is the demon worse than Agramon?"

"Yes. But not in the way you believe." Should I feel relieved? If so, I don't.

"Is it Lucifer?"

He scoffs, waving a hand to negate my words.

"Lucifer is a fallen angel, not a demon, and no, he is not the one we face."

"I thought he ruled Hell."

"Pride and Greed are more powerful. Lucifer rules, but not in the way I want."

Okay. Clearly Hell politics fly over my head. But I understand enough to know what he wants. My help to overthrow Pride and Greed. Since chances were good Rahab was the Pride he referred to, it meant the demon scarier than Agramon was Greed.

A little hard to believe, but whatever. Clearly Greed spooked Zagan worse than Agramon.

"And if I help you win, what happens? Do you rule Earth? Subjugate humans to your wishes? Kill me?"

Another negating hand wave. "Don't be ridiculous. I'd never kill you."

"Just turn me into your servant."

He smiles. "I will rule Hell, not Earth. Nothing would change on Earth. What difference would it matter to all these short-lived humans who the ruler of Hell is? Leadership changes. Rulers rise, rulers fall. Some rulers try too large of a power grab and need to be taken down. You would be helping clean up my home."

"And this would be advantageous to me, how?"

"You would help me. Helping me helps you. Not as many strong demons to fight. Wouldn't that be a good thing?"

I nod. Demons with lesser strength would make my job, the job of my fellow *Justitians*, easier. We could win more fights without dying, giving us more time to focus on minions who were more prominent on Earth than the demons, but did just as much, if not more, damage.

"Then you'll join me?"

I swallow. Willpower vanishes in the face of Zagan's persuasion. I want to do as he asks. I want him to be ruler of Hell. Through the *justitia's* memories, I know he has waited millennia for this chance, first by creating the *justitias*, then when the demon's control over the bracelets was broken, scheming to find a way to meet his goal. He needs me.

I want to help him.

"I will."

The expression on his face causes the hair on the back of my neck to stand on end. Did I make a mistake? Was agreeing to kill demons a mistake?

Nope, no way.

Zagan steps closer. I step back, hitting the counter, freezing as he moves to my side. One finger touches the mark on my neck, the mark he gave me, the mark he insists makes me his servant. My *justitia* slams shut my empathic pathway, keeping my brain from hemorrhaging at the demon's touch. Power flows from him into me, sinking deep, his red power I crave. The reservoir inside me fills, swelling with demonic power. The entity lying along my nerves shivers with pleasure. When Zagan removes his finger, my knees sag, and I catch myself on the counter.

"Together we will fight and together we will win. You are mine. Never forget it."

With a circular wave of his hand, he vanishes into a portal.

Breath flows from my lips in a whoosh of air. Nausea turns my stomach into a pit of fluttering flies. What did I agree to?

All good things. Help. Assistance. Aid. Killing demons.

Nothing wrong with any of those.

What would Smythe think of my promise to a demon? My agreeing to help with a major power shift in Hell? I can hear him already, a voice of disagreement despite the obvious "Less demons, more time to catch minions" benefits.

I tighten the robe's belt, drop my hands to my sides, and look up at the ceiling, as if the expanse gave answers.

It doesn't. I sigh. Helping Zagan was second nature. His plan made sense. Less powerful demons, more time to fight minions. Not to mention ridding the Agency of its demon.

All good things. Worthwhile goals.

Smythe would understand when I tell him.

Despite rationalizing my decision, despite knowing the hard choice I made benefited mankind the best, the heaviness in my chest coupled with my stomach turning into a sinking ball of lead only means one thing.

I sold my soul to the devil.

A word about the author…

Currently working on her urban fantasy series A Demon Huntress, Karilyn Bentley blends magic, dark fantasy, and romance mixed with a touch of funny that her readers expect and love.

Karilyn's love of reading stories and preference of sitting in front of a computer at home instead of in a cube, drove her to pen her own works. Her paranormal romance novella, *Werewolves in London*, placed in the Got Wolf contest and started her writing career as an author of sexy heroes and lush fantasy worlds.

Karilyn lives in Colorado with her own hunky hero, a crazy dog (a.k.a The Kraken), a funny puppy, and a handful of colorful saltwater fish. Find out more about Karilyn at www.karilynbentley.com

Thank you for purchasing
this publication of The Wild Rose Press, Inc.

If you enjoyed the story, we would appreciate your
letting others know by leaving a review.

For other wonderful stories,
please visit our on-line bookstore at
www.thewildrosepress.com.

For questions or more information
contact us at
info@thewildrosepress.com.

The Wild Rose Press, Inc.
www.thewildrosepress.com

Stay current with The Wild Rose Press, Inc.

Like us on Facebook

https://www.facebook.com/TheWildRosePress

And Follow us on Twitter
https://twitter.com/WildRosePress